JAGUAR'S PASSION

Guardians of the Fae Realms: Book 5

JL Madore

JL Madore

Cover Design: Gombar Cover Designs
Note: The moral right of the author has been asserted.

Jaguar's Passion: Guardians of the Fae Realms
JL Madore -- 1st ed.
ISBN: 978-1-989187-52-4

CHAPTER ONE

Calli

I circle the clearing, my flaming feathers flapping in the auburn and tangerine sky of sunset. With each lift and thrust of my massive wingspan, I ensure my flight doesn't go so high that I'll be noticed from a distance but high enough that I can say without a doubt, there's no portal gate here. No remnant magic tingles over my heated flesh. There's nothing that could be rebuilt or repaired to allow entry into the fae realm.

Dammit. My phoenix lets off a long squawk and then I meet Hawk's gaze and turn back. Another dead end. I should be getting used to it by now, but it still sucks. With the clearing below, I lean back and flex my talons at the ground.

Hawk's instructions for a smooth landing play back in my head: slow down, wings out, backward thrust, lean back, release my phoenix, and drop to my feet.

Easy for him to say. The ground always seems intent on coming at me and taking me out. That could be paranoia.

Whoa… wait… yikes…

Right before I hit the ground, I release my phoenix,

and I'm a woman once more. I don't stick the landing one hundy percent, but it's nothing a few running steps to catch my balance doesn't take care of.

I'll take it and call it a win.

At least I'm not skidding across fields and back lawns on my face anymore.

"Anything?" Kotah asks, meeting me with a flare of his never-ending optimism. My wolf is the spirit of our quint. He's all the hope and patience and beauty we could ever ask for in a mate. He's the youngest of the five of us, but in some ways, he is the old soul of the group. I think that comes from his native heritage and his connection to the natural world.

Or maybe it's his genius IQ.

Or his Omega gift coming through.

I meet his expectant gaze and remember he asked me if I found anything. "Oh, sorry, no. Nothing. I'm not picking up anything we could use."

He helps me into one of the new fireproof wrap dresses Hawk had made for me and I cover up. As a human turned wildling, I missed out on a few of the natural abilities they enjoy as preternatural perks.

I can't detect scents in the air like them. I don't have a bonded identity to my animal side like them—although they think that might develop with time. And I can't shed and re-manifest clothing like them.

When I shift, I either start naked and end naked or I start clothed and end naked because my clothing has gone up in flames. And where it used to take me days to regulate my body temperature back to normal, now it only takes ten or twelve hours, but that's still a long time to have to be naked when we're out and among other people.

Thank goodness for fireproof fabric.

"Don't look so dejected, Spitfire." Hawk steps out of his landing and flashes on black slacks and a black button-down dress shirt without breaking stride. He rolls the cuffs as he walks, and I don't think he even realizes how incredible I think that is. "We knew this would be a needle in the haystack endeavor. We've still got a dozen or so other sites to explore."

"Besides," Jaxx says, closing up the lawn chairs and tossing the lid on the cooler. "A good time was had by all. Brant, Kotah, and I got to sit here, shoot the breeze, and relax a bit while we watched you guys fly. Seein' your phoenix light up the sky steals our breath, kitten. It never gets old."

"You can say that again," Brant says. He picks up the cooler and lifts it into the open door of Hawk's Eurocopter AS365 Dauphin, a twin-engine, long-range luxury helicopter. "It's a good thing we're mated for life because I want to watch that until I'm an old and grizzly grizzly."

I chuckle and pull my hair free from the collar of my dress. Jaxx hands me a cider and I take a drink. It's unbelievably cold, but then again, it might be because my insides are still molten hot. I slip one foot behind the other and offer them a little curtsy. "Thank you. Thank you. I'm glad you boys enjoyed the show."

Kotah's smile is too cute. "We did. We talked about showing you how much but decided not to put Hawk's pilot through watching us get naked."

"Again," Brant chuckles.

Hawk sends them a look of pure censure and frowns. "Yes, thank you for your restraint. I'd rather not be flagged for that HR complaint twice in one month. That last afternoon delight cost me twenty grand in pain and suffering."

"Pain and sufferin' my dimpled behind," Jaxx says. "You never should've paid that one out. That guy was just mad he didn't get an invite to join the party."

I chuckle and send Hawk a sympathetic smile.

Brant and Jaxx finish packing up our belongings and then Hawk offers me a hand and helps me inside the helicopter. My seat is covered with a fire blanket, just in case, and I settle in for the ride. "What's our next stop?"

Jaxx highlights our current position with a red swipe. "That's it for today. Time to head back to the palace."

Kotah falls noticeably quiet at the mention of going back there, but there's not much to be done about it. As the new Fae Prime, his coronation ceremony isn't something we can skip.

Although we totally would if we could.

"I have a suggestion for the four of you." Hawk slides the door closed and seals us in before settling on the bench seat at the back of the helicopter across from me. "In light of Kotah's hatred of life in the palace and his recent brush with death by poison, I wondered about having a private residence on the grounds of the Bastion. There's no getting around the times we'll have to go to the palace, but when we do, we don't have to stay there."

Kotah frowns. "And we'd live at the Bastion?"

"No. I'm hoping that once things settle down, we'll

split our time between the Northwood property and the place I'm building in New Jersey."

"That's very thoughtful of you, Hawk," I say. Everything Hawk does, has a great deal of thought behind it. People on the outside looking in might find him calculating, but when that power is used with us, it's always about trying to fill our every need. "What do you think, Kotah?"

He shakes his head. "It *is* very thoughtful—and I appreciate it—but you can't buy or build a house everywhere we go."

Hawk's gaze clouds with confusion. "Why not? I have more money than we'll ever need and I want the four of you to be safe and happy."

Kotah unbuckles his seatbelt and gestures to switch spots with Brant. Taking a seat next to our corporate romantic, Kotah leans sideways and kisses him. "Thank you for worrying about me. I appreciate that you will do anything within your power to make things more palatable for me, but I'm solidly in 'suck it up' territory now. Until changes are made, I need to stay at the palace and assume my place. Once I've established myself and have a firm grasp on what I want, we'll revisit this and discuss moving."

"We can always escape for a weekend now and then, and hang in the bunker," Brant says. "We never did finish our game of Margarita madness."

Jaxx laughs. "That's because Calli got drunk and seduced me. We definitely need a do-over on that one."

I laugh. "If I get a vote, I like the idea of making our home base at the Northwood property. North Dakota is where I felt the most at home, so far."

Hawk frowns. "Of course, you get a vote, Spitfire. What say the rest of you?"

"Yeah, me too," Brant says. "Kotah's land in North Dakota felt like a good fit for all of us."

Jaxx smiles. "And Brant, Hawk, and I got left out of the skinny dippin' in the grotto. We gotta get back to at least even the scales of justice on that front."

Hawk nods. "Okay, we won't make any decisions just yet but the offer is always open. The Bastion has secure grounds, a bit more nature to enjoy, and since I'm already rebuilding the cabin that blew up with you four in it, I'll make a few upgrades to make it feel more like home."

"Perfect. Then we know it's an option," Kotah says. "Once the coronation ceremony is over and we vet the Fae Council to get them up and running again, we'll talk about where we want to live. Who knows, if the place we find to make the new portal gate is in Alaska, maybe we move closer to the front lines of fae integration."

Jaxx frowns. "Then if we're throwing out random states, I'm hoping we can establish a portal gate in Arizona or New Mexico. I don't know about you guys, but this jaguar likes heat against his fur."

I laugh. "This phoenix is rather fond of heat too."

Brant, Kotah, and Hawk all chuckle. Hawk nods. "Okay, then, let's hope that wherever we can establish a portal gate there's heat."

Jaxx

It's after eight when Hawk's pilot lands us on the front lawn of the palace and we call our exploration over. We didn't find anything promising at any of the locations listed of past portal gate sites, but we take it in stride. The five of us are healthy and happy and for now, that's enough.

"Welcome home, kids," Mama says, as we come through the door of the Timber Trails suite in the Fae Palace. Our two-story residence smells divine, the heavenly scent of my mother's cooking filling the air with both the ambrosia of home cooking and her love.

"Hey, Mama." I lean in and kiss her cheek. "You're spoiling us."

Her indulgent smile is home to me. Always has been. "I figured y'all might be tired from your travels and wouldn't feel like cooking, so I took some liberties. Everything is ready for the table. Enjoy. We'll meet up for brunch tomorrow to hear all about it and discuss the next steps."

"Thank you, Mama," Kotah says, dropping his duffle inside the door to head straight over to hug her. "It smells delicious. Thank you for all you do."

Mama cups his cheeks and plants a lipstick kiss on his forehead. "You're welcome, my sweet boy."

Daddy takes my bag and Calli's and walks them to the top of the stairs. When he comes back, he gathers Mama and ushers her toward the door. "Enjoy your evening, kids. We're across the hall if you need us."

"Thank you, Jonathan," Hawk says. "Good night, Maggie. Dinner smells wonderful."

I kiss Mama once more on the way out, squeeze Daddy's hand, and then lock the door behind them.

"They are the two nicest people I've ever met,"

Hawk says, untying the laces on his boots. "I can't even tell you how many times I've felt unworthy to have your parents caring for me. It's humbling."

I wave that away and hold up the ring box Mama slipped me on her way out. "You're worthy, hotness. Change those internal tapes. We all deserve each other. The universe decided and it's a slam dunk. And to prove my point… we have something for you."

Hawk waggles his brow, but he knows what's coming. He should, he bought the mating bands we all wear.

Calli lets off a squeal of excitement and slides an arm around my waist. "Okay, so, you left the engraving of your ring up to us and it was a no-brainer. Wasn't it, guys?"

Kotah nods and moves Hawk to stand in front of us. "We went with your theme and continued the sentiment. Our soul, Our strength, Our passion, Our fire, and…"

I open the ring box and let Kotah do the honors. The kid has been on cloud nine since we all got our mating bands and with all the turmoil and strife in his life, we let him take his happiness where he can.

"Hawk Barron, we declare you, Our heart."

Hawk chuckles. "Really?"

Brant arches a brow and pulls the leather tie from his hair. The chestnut waves fall loose and settle across his broad shoulders. "You sound surprised."

"Honestly, I am. I've always considered my heart as cold, dark, and hardened. I didn't realize you saw things so differently."

Calli steps forward, hugs him, and then presses her

hand against his chest. "Your heart may have been hardened but it's far from cold and dark. You prove that to us every day."

When she pushes up on her toes to lay a kiss on him, Hawk's arms wrap around her. She may have meant it as a moment of simple affection, but as things go with us, it gets hot and heavy faster than we can control.

I groan as Hawk's hips grind forward and his hold on her ass rucks up the hem of her dress. Calli has an amazing ass. "And just like that, I'm hard and randy," I growl. "Dayam, are we ever gonna get a handle on this mating hunger?"

Brant chuckles, adjusting the lay of his cock in his jeans. "Fuck, I hope not, Jaguar. Why ruin a good thing?"

"A great thing," Kotah corrects.

Calli crosses the line of restraint first by reaching down and palming the ridge filling out the front of Hawk's slacks. "Can dinner hold for a bit? I'm hungry to feast on something else right now."

I check the oven, turn everything off, and cover everything on the stove. "All good to sate your hunger, kitten. Have at him."

She practically rips Hawk's designer pants open, greedy to get at him. You gotta love our mate. She loves sucking cock and isn't about to apologize for it.

Which is SAF. Sexy. As. Fuck.

Calli pushes Hawk against the edge of the kitchen table and bends to take him into her mouth.

He arches back, and his entire body shudders in a racking wave of pleasure as her lips split over his crown and he sinks into the hot depths of her mouth. “Yeah, Spitfire. Whatever you’re hungry for. Devour away.”

“Oh, this is on,” Brant says, reaching over his head to pull his shirt off.

Yep, it doesn’t take much to set our horny quint off on a sexual tangent. Not that I’m complaining. Yeah-no, that will never happen.

“Be right back.” Kotah jogs off to the bathroom.

Brant’s got his shirt off and is shifting in behind Calli’s ass. The corded muscles that run up and down his back flex as he moves, and sexy hot anticipation burns in my balls. “You know what I love most about these wrap dresses, beautiful?”

Calli’s too busy deep-throating Hawk to answer.

I chuckle, toss my shirt, and undo my pants. They fall to the floor in a quiet flop and I step free. “Tell us, Bear.”

He bends and reaches around Calli’s waist, pulling the end of the tie holding the two sides of the fabric together. The fabric unwraps from her waist and peels away from her shoulders. He tosses it to the back of the couch, leaving her gloriously naked. “It’s a one and done outfit.”

“Well done, Bear.” Hawk’s voice is deep and husky, his breath quickening. “I would’ve done the honors if I wasn’t currently holding myself up.”

“A little weak in the knees, are you, hotness?”

Hawk glances over and I stroke off for him. My cock is hard and demanding I get in the game by starting with a little light teasing. “Make him come hard, kitten. Teach him that it’s fun when the predator becomes the prey."

Hawk sends me a searing gaze and I close the distance. "Twist his sac." I continue to palm my cock for Hawk's pleasure. "He loves it when I play rough with his balls, don't you, Avian?"

"I do," he says, his chest rising, his breathing quick.

Calli's arm shifts between their bodies and *shiiit*, I can feel the surge of sensation from here. Hawk shouts out, his fingers gripping the edge of the table like he's holding on for dear life. Which, having been there more than once with Calli, he most definitely is.

Brant is bent over Calli's back, one hand occupied with her tits while the other is busy rubbing her core.

"Can I help you with these, big guy?" I reach around his hips, take control of his button fly, and strip him down. He steps out of his jeans and I run my hands down his massive thighs. The man is a breathtaking specimen of honed muscle and power held in reserve.

And he's mine for the taking.

Kotah comes back as Hawk's head tips back and our corporate raider barks a triumphant cry of a great orgasm. Damn, he's sexy. Fully dressed in his fancy black dress shirt and his pants pooled around his ankles, his chest heaves as he loses himself in her mouth.

We've all learned how much Calli gets off on oral.

I don't know how it affects the other guys but knowing she relishes swallowing my cum down pretty much wrecks me every time. "How was that for an appetizer, kitten?"

Calli straightens, brushing her finger against her lip, claiming every drop. "Perfect. Just what I wanted."

"Time for the rest of us to eat," Brant says, lifting her and laying her out on the kitchen table. "I think we should all enjoy a feast."

As Brant opens Calli's legs and drops his head, I get an inspired idea. "Mhmm, I like the way you think, big guy. Kotah, help me with something, will you?"

Kotah follows me to the stove and I pull out the roasting pan. Mama has already sliced the meat and drained the juice to make the gravy. Awesome. "Bring the potatoes and the gravy. If Brant wants a feast, I think we should all have one. How about you?"

Kotah

"Whatever you say, Jaxx." I'm never sure what crazy idea Jaxx has in mind but he's never let us down. I grab the pot of mashed potatoes, the one with gravy, and a few serving spoons out of the container on the counter. "Where do you want it?"

Calli is splayed across the kitchen table with Brant's mouth buried in her core.

Hawk has finished stripping off his clothes and seems to know exactly what Jaxx has in mind. "Fuck yeah. Great idea."

"Blindfold?"

"Definitely."

Hawk launches off the ground and takes flight in his hawk form. He flies up over the railing of the second floor and is back a moment later with a red, satin blindfold.

Where Jaxx sets the roasting pan down, I line up my pots. When he takes off the lid, I do the same.

"The name of the game is Mate Feast," Jaxx says. "Hawk, would you do the honors?"

"My pleasure." Hawk shifts to the head of the table, kisses Calli, and gets her blindfolded.

Brant is taking his time, licking, and nuzzling her moist folds. "As long as I don't have to stop, I'm in."

Jaxx's grin widens. "Oh, no. There's no stopping. Let me enhance your feasting experience." He takes a small slice of roast beef and places it on Calli's mons.

"Oh my, that's warm," Calli says, her nipples peaking. "And yep, dripping right into—"

Brant growls and devours the meat, licking her with earnest. "Please, sir. I want some more."

"Coming right up." Jaxx, sets to work lining up the slices of roast beef from Calli's sternum down to her core. The meat juices drip down her hips and ribs and she squirms a little, but—guessing by the accompanying feminine groan—it's in a good way.

Jaxx sets out another slice for our bear and Brant dives in to devour her once again.

Jaxx, Hawk, and I focus on laying out our platter for our feast. I'm in charge of the carrots and corn and Hawk takes mashed potatoes.

"It takes a bit of strategy to get these veggies not to roll off with her chest heaving," I say, after finally securing them in a nest of mashed potatoes over her naval.

"Look. I'm an artist," Hawk says, pointing to Calli's breasts. They're each heaped with mashed potatoes with a baby carrot sticking up in the center. "I call it an ode to Calli's delicious tits."

"It's perfect." Jaxx scoops one of the large serving spoons filled with gravy and his grin widens. "Now for the final touch."

He pours a long line of rich, brown gravy from her throat to her sternum, circling both breasts, and then down the meat lining the center of her body, to the mashed potatoes and veggies at her naval and then down to Brant's mouth.

After setting aside the pots and pan, Jaxx gestures to the delicious mess we've made.

"Let the Mate Feast begin."

CHAPTER TWO

Brant

I fucking love my life… and not because I'm balls deep inside my mate with a full belly and my retinas being overloaded with all manner of mate fuckery. Okay, that has a lot to do with it, but not all. When the universe fated the five of us to become the Phoenix Quint, I won the fucking lottery.

Ha! I also won the *fucking* lottery.

Jaxx's Mate Feast was a huge success. Calli came apart five or six times and we let our animal sides ascend to have fun. After we finished feeding off her, Jaxx and Kotah took pity on her and hand-fed her until she was full as well.

Once our queen's needs were met, we came upstairs to hit the showers.

When Kotah renovated the suite, here in the palace, he had the foresight to have a five-person shower built in the master ensuite. It boasts adjustable jet sprayers—that Hawk is currently playing with—a seat in one corner—which Jaxx and Kotah are enjoying—and a ledge to lean over on the opposite wall—that's where I have Calli propped to give me the best possible access. It also has all manner of aptly placed handles which we love to make use of.

The entire setup is built for group sex shenanigans. I expect Hawk had a strong hand in the design. Fist-bump to them both because… yeah, good times.

Glancing down, I watch my cock glisten as I pull back to my tip and then slide deep into Calli's heat.

Water cascading down bare flesh is hella sexy.

My girl has her belly resting on the ledge and her hands pressed flat against the granite wall beyond. The cantilevered plane saves her legs from having to support her and gives me the time to penetrate her in a slow and steady pace from behind for as long as I please.

I could live and die doing this for the rest of my life and be happy… except the tightening of her insides means I won't get that wish. Once Calli's muscles get greedy, her release is soon to ignite. "Fuck I love how hard you grip my cock before you come."

"Preach," Jaxx says, his head dropped back as Kotah sucks him off. The jaguar is sitting on the corner seat with one hand resting on Kotah's head in his lap, and the other hand fondling Hawk's balls while the avian strokes off to the view.

Calli's legs start to quiver and her throaty pant signals the first crest of her orgasm wave. I grip her hips tighter and thrust deep. I'm big—sometimes I worry too big for her—but when she's well stretched by the others and has had a few orgasms like now, she can take all of me.

"That's it, beautiful," I rasp. "Take all of me. Feel

me fill you and rub your insides."

"I do. It's so good… give me more."

My bear growls deep in my chest and I give my girl her wish. "Brace yourself, baby."

It doesn't take long. Her core is already pulsing when I pick up the pace. Once I drop the caution and really hammer into her, she shatters. Over the past months, we've all been getting to know each other's preferences.

Calli likes to be fucked hard through her orgasms… and if the stars align and you wind her up just right…

"Gawd, yes."

"Fuck, yes," Hawk says as her body bursts into the glow of her flaming female.

When her wild side ignites, all bets are off. Her second-level orgasm rips through her and I unhinge my hips. Hard and fast I penetrate her, hitting home with bruising force. My thighs are on fire, but I love the burn.

This is what Calli loves.

When she's shattering in this form, she needs everything we've got.

Jaxx grunts, arches back, and his hips start to kick.

I meet his gaze and he's totally getting off on both Kotah's attention and seeing me hammer Calli's wild side.

His purr rips loose and fills the steamy air.

Bastard.

I meet Hawk's gaze and yeah, that purr does me in too. Hawk and I lose control and it's orgasms all around. As I spill into our mate, I watch the creamy streams of cum shoot over Hawk's hand. He's stroking off hard and the result of his labors is getting washed into the drain. With a hand braced against the glass wall, his body constricts and his muscles convulse.

Sometimes I need more hands so I can play with all the things I want at once.

I ride out my release, close my eyes, and try to remember how to breathe. The closed-in space is saturated in the mixed scents of our sweat, combined orgasms, and our hunger for one another. The carnal aromas blend to produce a heady, drugging effect.

Yeah, like I said… I love my life.

Hawk

I wake sometime in the middle of the night to a gentle rocking on the bed beside me. Who could possibly still be horny after the sexcapades we all got up to before crashing? I chuckle and pry one eye open, surprised to see Kotah palming himself.

"Hey," I whisper. "You good?"

The guilty look he flashes me stands as one of the only times he's looked his age. "Sorry. I'll stop."

"Don't stop on my account. I was just surprised you've got anything left."

He shrugs. "It's a nervous habit I got into as a teen."

"You're worried about the coronation tomorrow?"

He nods. "It's fine. Go back to sleep. I'm just keyed up."

One look in those dark chocolate eyes tells me the one thing my wolf is not, is fine. "Do you mind if I help you with your nervous habit?"

Kotah's mouth quirks up in a crooked smile. "I

don't mind if you don't."

Damn, this kid squeezes my heart. Lifting the sheet, I climb over his hip and settle in behind him. "I do my best work with my right hand."

He lifts his head and I move his hair to slide my arm under his neck. Spooning him, I snuggle in tight and reach over his hip with my other hand to relieve him from his palm duties. "Never be embarrassed about needing an outlet. I've used sex as every outlet imaginable. I've got you."

He snuggles his ass into the cradle of my hips and my cock jumps at the attention. The friction of skin-on-skin when my mate is naked, in my arms, and needs comforting is nothing I can ignore. That doesn't mean I need to address it. This is about comforting him, not me taking my pleasures.

"Anything you need—ever—all you have to do is ask."

I lift my bottom arm off the mattress, across his chest, and grip his shoulder. I'm quite a bit taller than Kotah which works well when I want to surround him with my body. While I stroke his shaft, base to tip, I kiss his shoulder and close my eyes, lost in the rapture of him being mine.

The guy is perfect, his body young and fit, his skin so soft it seems unreal. He's got the heart of a saint and the inner strength to be anyone's moral compass.

And he's mine.

"I love you, Kotah. Just close your eyes and let me make you feel good. I've got you, now, tomorrow, and always."

Calli

I get up with Hawk first thing and leave the others to sleep. I don't like it when he leaves us and goes off to live his business life knowing we're all still snuggly and warm without him. He's made such great strides in merging with the group, I want to protect and nurture that.

Since Hawk completed mating with the others, he's taken his suppressant pill and slept with us every night. He's even talked to the doctor about taking a half-dose now that he's working through some of his dark baggage.

Jaxx and Brant assured him if anything happens, they'll step in and keep everyone safe.

I honestly believe him working through his Daddy issues is freeing him and he'll get to a point he won't need to take medication at all. Still, if he does, that's fine too. Whatever it takes to eliminate the protective barriers between us.

The two of us leave Jaxx, Kotah, and Brant in the master bedroom and pad quietly to the adjoining room. The guys moved our dressers in here to give us more room in the master. It also makes it easier for us to get dressed in the mornings without disturbing the others.

Hawk's clothes are mostly hung in the closet, so he heads there, and I go for the drawers of my dresser. After our group shower last night, we're good to dress and go. I pull on a matching panty and bra set, a pair of stretchy, brushed denim jeans, and a cream, cable-knit sweater. It's a home day until we have to get ready for the coronation, so comfy clothes for the win.

Hawk pulls on a pair of black boxers and then decks

himself out in his usual GQ corporate attire. No complaints. With his tats and the fine clothes and his sleeves rolled up as he does… yummm.

"What?" he says, pressing a hand on his buttons and turning to check himself in the mirror. "Am I lopsided? You're staring."

I chuckle. "No sexy man. I was drinking you in. You're breathtaking and I like the view."

He relaxes and pulls me against his chest. "And I like taking your breath away."

"I like that too."

He slides a hand beneath my hair and grips the nape of my neck. Without apology, he pulls me close and takes possession of my mouth. Hawk kisses with the same fervor and passion he uses to tackle life.

He's the boss and he'll take care of everything.

And he does.

It doesn't take long before my heart is racing, and my mind is flip-flopping between not getting swept away and tossing reality to the side and jumping him.

But he has work to do and almost lost control of his company while being distracted by us. I won't let that happen again.

I ease back and smile, taking a moment to catch my breath. "Good morning, to you too."

His smug grin is too sexy. "So, what's your plan for this morning, beautiful mate of mine?"

He takes my hand and together we take our exit and walk along the second-floor balcony toward the stairs. "I was thinking of baking those cinnamon buns Mama put into our freezer and looking through the texts she sent over on the initial set up and deconstruction of the portal gates. Brant, Jaxx, and I were talking yesterday about how they were originally created. Maybe if we can't restore one, we can create one."

"I can't imagine where we'd get that kind of power, but yeah, leave no stone unturned."

We descend the open staircase, hand-in-hand, and my stomach lets off an insistent growl. "Now that I'm thinking about those cinnamon buns, I'm getting ravenous."

Hawk chuckles. "It's a good thing we're wildlings. Without dual metabolisms, you and I would never be able to get off the ground the way Jaxx's mother feeds us. Brant can afford to be heavy and dense. We're birds. That's entirely different."

I smile. "After the Mate Feast last night, I'll never complain about Maggie preparing food for us. That was an all-time highlight for me… something I'll likely replay in my mind for ages."

"You and me both, Spitfire. You and me both."

Thanks to the timer on the machine, the coffee is hot and freshly brewed. "Are you having your special French Press this morning or joining me for regular java?"

"I'll join you."

I grab us each a mug from the cupboard, splash a bit of coconut milk in the bottom of his, and drop a square of chocolate in mine. The two of us get made fun of by Jaxx and Brant who are coffee traditionalists, but we've decided they don't know what they're missing.

After pouring two full mugs, I set them on the counter of the breakfast bar, and he takes over. His spoon lets off a soft *tink, tink, tink* as he stirs our coffees, while I get the cinnamon buns out to thaw. When that's done, the two of us take our morning jolt of caffeine into the office.

"What's on the sexy CEO's agenda this morning?"

He checks his watch. "Jayne and I are still fielding the damage done by my father. She's been going through all our active projects and interactions with clients. I'm still catching up on what I neglected." He pulls his mug down from his mouth and pegs me with a worried gaze. "Sorry. I didn't mean to bring her up. That was thoughtless."

I sit at the desk opposite his and jiggle the mouse to wake up my screen. "Onward and upward. If she keeps her catty bitch claws in and her hands off the merchandise I can deal. The important thing is that you reclaim your company."

His brow creases. "Are you serious about that or being generous on my behalf?"

I think about that and shrug. "Both. The mating magic pulled the rug out from under her and she reacted badly. I can relate because I did too. Her kneejerk reaction leveled me. Mine leveled Jaxx. It would be petty and hypocritical of me to punish you and jeopardize your company because she devolved into total territorial bitch mode."

The hope glimmering in his steel-gray eyes takes me by surprise. "If you're serious, I'd be beyond relieved. I've been trying to figure out how to sever her from the company, but with my focus shifting to you and the others, I can't see how the FCO can continue without her there to pick up my slack. I thought I might have to shut down."

I don't want that. His company is a huge part of his identity and accomplishments in life. "So, if I'm serious, we get you and she gets the headache of an infiltrated company?"

"Basically, yes."

I take another few sips of my chocolatey coffee and nod. "I can live with that."

"Seriously? I don't want you to say that if you don't mean it. You're a thousand times more important to me than Jayne. I'll shut the FCO down before I lose you over her."

"Oh, you'll never lose me, boss man."

"And thank the Powers for that." His relief is all the reward I need. Taking the high road might suck in the future but it's worth it. "Thanks, Spitfire. I owe you one—a huge one."

"I know how you can thank me properly."

He straightens in his seat, the corner of his mouth lifting in a crooked smile. "Oh, I like the sound of this. Lay it on me. What can I do?"

"I want a turn in the Den of Debachury with you. You've taken Jaxx and Brant in there and I asked first. It bugs me that Jayne's played with that side of you, but you won't share him with me."

His brow tightens and as I watch, those steel-gray eyes cloud over. "You don't think... Don't compare what Jayne and I did to what you and I share. It's worlds apart."

"How can I not. It's apples to apples. We are both women you've been with and yet she got all of you and I get only the parts you think I can handle."

"She didn't get *all* of me," he snaps, standing and leaning into his fists on the desk. "She never got my love or my devotion. I never adored her or wanted to build a future with her. Jayne and I were about work and burning off stress. You are about everything I live and breathe for."

"Then I don't understand why you won't take me in there with you. We've always had fun with sexplay. Why do Jaxx and Brant rank and I don't?"

He huffs and rounds the desks to stand in front of me. "What if I don't want to show you that side of me? Maybe I'm not ready."

"Why? I know who you are. I accept you and love you no matter what? I'm not going to judge and I'm certainly not worried about me."

He nods. "I get that you think that… I just… can I protect our love a little longer? I don't want anything to change yet. I don't want to be like that with you… at least not yet."

As disappointed as I am, I think I understand. For people like us, who fought and scraped for everything, to have everything we ever wanted is scary as hell.

He's waiting for the shoe to drop.

"Okay. For now, we'll play it your way. Just know that it's something both Kotah and I are looking forward to."

He rakes through his hair with rough fingers and sighs. "I don't know why that is such a big deal to you two. Honestly, I love the sex we've been having."

"So do I but it's a part of you that you won't share

with us. We want all of you."

A text bings in on his phone, but he doesn't look over. He's solely focused on me, his internal struggle palpable. "I promise it's not about keeping you two at a distance. I love you both and love who I am with you without all the things BDSM and hard kink bring into play. Does that make sense?"

I didn't mean to get heavy with him right before he has to navigate a day of corporate minefields. I've told the guys not to push him. Just let him grow and get his footing.

Now I'm the one pushing him off balance.

Stepping into his arms, I hug him and press my cheek to his silky dress shirt. "It's fine. Forget I brought it up."

"No. Don't do that," he says, his voice a low growl.

I ease back and look up at him. "Do what? I agreed with you. I don't want it to be a thing between us."

He sighs. "But don't negate what you want because we're not on the same page. Just give me time to work through my insecurities."

I brush my lips over his and smile. "As it happens, we have time. I'm not going anywhere, and neither are you."

"And thank fuck for that." He drops his head and presses his forehead to mine. "I hear you and I'm working on things."

I kiss him again and this time when the text notification bings, I step back and hand him his phone. "Enough talk. Get to work, slacker."

He takes the phone and clasps my hand. "Are we

okay?"

I smile. "Oh, baby, we're so far beyond okay it blows my mind. You work and I'll bake. I'll be back in a while with some cinnamon seduction."

CHAPTER THREE

Jaxx

Calli's in the office with Hawk when I come down to get things started in the kitchen. Heightened hearing isn't always a blessing. I don't mean to hear their conversation, but I do. The fact that my mates are still struggling to completely lock down makes me hurt for them. It will happen, I don't doubt that for a second, but it still hurts.

"Hey, kitten. Good morning." I round the island, capture her in my arms, and hug her tight. My cat lets off a long purr of contentment and she relaxes into my embrace. When I'm sure she's feeling a bit more grounded, I ease back and point to the tray of sugary wonder thawing on the counter. "I take it you have a hankerin' for sweet this mornin'."

She climbs up onto one of the island stools and smiles. "Yeah. Your mother's cinnamon bliss is hard not to crave."

"True enough. Do you want to do it, or can I take over in the kitchen?"

"Not *it*." She chuckles and raises her hands. "Riley

and I fought almost every day over who had to make the next meal. If you want to take the reins, be my guest."

I turn the oven to pre-heat, spray a glass pan, and get to work. "Speakin' of your mysterious bestie, have you had any cranium conversations lately?"

She shakes her head. "No, and I'm surprised. I thought it was because here at the palace we are the closest to the connection point between the two realms, but now, nothing."

"Maybe that's because Hawk's daddy blew up that connection."

"Maybe. If that's the reason, all we have to do is comb the entire nation and if Riley talks to me, we know we're close to a prospective spot."

I chuckle. "Oh, is that all. I'll tell Lukas to get the bus tuned up for our road trip."

"Road trip?" Kotah says, jogging down the stairs with Brant. "Are we on the move?"

"I wish," Calli says, recounting the conversation to bring Brant and Kotah up to speed. "If our lives were our own and time meant nothing, I can't imagine anything better than the five of us meandering the world in our tour bus of bliss."

The temperature gauge beeps on the oven and I slide the rolls in to bake. After setting the timer, I pull out the eggs, peppers, mushrooms, and milk. "Kotah, do you want to play brunch buddies and cook with me?"

His face lights up and I give myself a solid point for putting that look on his face on a day I know he has dreaded his entire life.

"You're becoming quite the chef in your own right,"

Calli says, squeezing his hand. "I thought maybe tonight we could shut the world away and you could treat us to a round of your pulled chicken nachos."

Kotah smiles. "I look forward to it more than you know."

Brant pats his belly. "We'll look forward to it too, buddy. Something to focus on through the trials of the day. I'm thinking we challenge Jaxx to come up with a drinking game to accompany the nachos. Hopefully, something that ends with us all being naked."

I laugh. "All my drinking games end with us naked."

"Yes, they do—"

"Knock, knock," Daddy says from the hall. "Parental ears on the other side of the door."

I roll my eyes as Calli, Brant, and Kotah all bust up laughing. Strolling over to the door, I unlock things and usher them inside. Daddy's laughing. Mama pats my hot cheeks and giggles. "Naked is good, baby boy. No need to blush."

I'm shutting the door when Doc and Keyla come out of the suite up the hall. By the wide-eyes they flash me, I get the sense that they didn't mean for me to catch Keyla coming out of his room first thing. Busted.

"You guys joining for brunch?"

Keyla looks to Doc for the answer and he shrugs and nods. "Sure. I could eat."

I laugh. "You're a bear. You boys can always eat." Before I shut the door this time, I take a last look. The only person we're missing is Lukas. I'm not sure if he's back from cleansing the portal site yet or not. He's not in the hall though, so I'm good to get back inside.

"Good morning, all," Keyla says. She hugs her brother and Kotah holds onto her longer than usual. Damn, I wish I could take the weight of this stupid Fae Prime position from him. Sadly, it isn't my burden to bear.

"We're going to get through today, Wolf," I say. "One hour at a time and as a family."

"Definitely as a family, son," Daddy says, meeting his gaze across the kitchen. "That's how we Stanton's do things. Now, let's spend the day together and forget about things for a few more hours."

Kotah

"It's just a day," I say, staring at the reflection of my sister in the mirror. The hours with the Stantons went by too fast and now there's nothing to be done but get ready to face my duties as the Fae Prime. "I'll get through this one, horrid day, and then I have my whole life with my mates ahead of me."

"Exactly," Keyla says, her fingers skimming through the lengths of my hair as she plaits it in the ceremonial fashion for our people. "It doesn't matter who says what before, during, or after the ceremony because by sundown tonight, it's over and you're the man."

I chuckle. "You should be the man. You were always better suited for navigating the inroads of prime duties."

"But you have the penis."

I roll my eyes. "That's so stupid."

"But that's the way of things. It's okay. Everything happens as it's meant to. Someday soon, the logic of things will become clear and we will see why this isn't my destiny. For some reason, this is all you." When her braiding meets the ends of my hair, she reaches over my shoulder.

I pass her the leather tie and try to draw breath through stiff lungs. "A leader must embrace his duty—despite personal sentiment, obstacles, dangers, or pressures from others. To fail in this is to lose the honor of being a male of worth."

"How many times did Father try to castrate you with those words?"

"Too many times to count." I think about my father and our relationship both through my childhood and at the end of his life. If I am ever blessed to have young, my child will know to the marrow of his or her bones that I love them more than my own life. I'll never do what our parents did to us. "Will you do my war paint?"

"War paint, eh? That's dramatic."

"It's how I feel. It's how I've always felt."

"Then yes. I'll get you painted and ready for battle."

"Thanks."

She leans against my back and wraps her arms around me. "I love you, Kotah. You are my big brother and my best friend and my hero—but just so you know, you'll never be my king and I'll kick your ass if you try."

I exhale and smile. "Thank you."

Hawk

It's after one when Jaxx catches me out on the balcony

having a smoke. "Hey," he says, "are you ready to join us? Keyla's up getting Kotah ready. I think he could use some time with all four of us before it's time to go downstairs."

I take a long pull on my cigarette and try to settle my nerves. "My computer is off and I'm gathering myself for what's to come. It guts me that he's being forced into something he so desperately doesn't want."

Jaxx sidles up beside me and confiscates my smoke. Putting it to his lips, he inhales and lets his eyes roll closed. "Damn, I needed that."

"Too bad it doesn't do more than take the edge off."

"It's enough," he takes another long draw and blows out a breath of exotic smelling smoke. "Listen… I know you're accustomed to bein' the alpha and the Dom and the CEO, so I know what the loss of control is doin' to you. I'll say to you the same thing I said to Kotah. We'll get through today, one hour at a time, and as a family."

He hands me my cigarette back and I finish it off and butt out. "Thanks, puss."

"My pleasure." He opens his arms and meets me chest to chest. Holding me tight, he speaks close to my ear. "Having faith in love is new to you, so follow my lead on this. It's going to be fine. We'll make it fine for him. No matter what comes, we'll cover his ass."

I close my eyes and images of my private moment with Kotah in the night fill my head. "And what a fine ass he has."

Jaxx's chest bounces against mine and he steps back with a Cheshire grin lighting up his face. "No shit. One look at that body and I'm hard and horny."

I laugh and adjust my cock behind the zipper of my dress pants. "Okay, stop or I'll be tenting at the royal coronation."

Jaxx nods holding the door open for us to head back inside. "I'm sure that's on an etiquette list of what not to do at a Fae Prime event."

"I'm sure." When I pass him, I brush my hand across the front of his pants and find the solid length I suspected I would. "Ha, at least I won't be the only one black-listed."

"Nope. I'll be right there with you in exile."

Calli

In the almost three months since I resurrected as the Phoenix of the Fae Realm, I've learned tons about species and expectations and lore. None of it prepared me for the magnitude of what it means for Kotah to take his place as the Fae Prime.

He's dressed in traditional warrior leathers and a wolf-pelt cape with a thirty-foot train. His hair is braided all fancy, and his beautiful face is unrecognizable beneath a dramatic mask of colors. It breaks my heart.

Nothing about this is Kotah.

Traditionally, the Prime's mate walks up the aisle of the outdoor auditorium on his right arm. We discussed me filling that spot but Kotah wouldn't hear of it. No mate left behind. I take his right arm and Jaxx is to my right. Hawk is on his left arm and Brant to his left.

We are the Phoenix Quint, and no one will leave here not knowing it. Even if anyone had something to say about it, what would it matter—the magic of the fae universe chose us.

Suck it, critics.

The distance from the ceremonial entrance of the palace out to the auditorium is about three times the length of the red carpet outside the Academy Awards.

Growing up in California, Riley and I went a couple of times to watch the rich and famous walk the walk.

Never in a million did I think it would be me someday. And certainly, I never could've dreamed I'd be walking the walk with my four wildling husbands.

Mind. Blown.

"Too bad we didn't get a turnout," Brant says.

I'm not sure if he's joking or not until I see Jaxx fighting a smile. Okay, I thought he was kidding because there are thousands of people here.

"Behave, Bear," Hawk says.

"And if I don't?" the suggestive tone goes unanswered but our bear's smart-ass strategy hits home. Kotah's gait becomes marginally less stiff and I think part of him finds Brant's insouciance charming.

When we get to the end of the line, we climb a ramp to a raised dais. The officiant of the ceremony is there, standing in emerald robes looking pompous, to his right is a private seating area with the eleven members of the Fae Council, to his left is the private seating area with Kotah's mother, sister, Raven, Doc, and Jaxx's parents. Straight back and behind the officiant stands a massive pyre.

The wooden platform rises eight feet off the dais and is topped with a wooden totem of a man lying in state. Even made of wood, the realistic rendering of the man is quite impressive. I never met him, but it doesn't take a genius to realize that it's Kotah's father.

"Is that a sarcophagus kinda thing?"

Jaxx leans closer and whispers. "No, kitten. Wildling bodies are lain out in the wilds of forest or field to be consumed by wildlife. The Prime's body would've been returned into the forest to reassimilate into the cycle of life by now. This is representational."

Gross. "Do I have to be eaten? Is there an opt-out?"

Before Jaxx can answer, the officiant comes forward and starts the ceremony. He asks the dignitaries and guests to please take their seats and then gestures with his hands for Jaxx and I and Hawk and Brant to move to the sides.

We take the cue and leave poor Kotah alone as the center of attention. Gripping Jaxx's hand, I reach into myself and find the mating bond tethering us to Kotah. Taking hold of it, I send him as much love and strength as I can.

I smile as Hawk slides his hand into Brant's and the others follow suit. No one else can see or feel it, but privately, the five of us have shut out the world and are having a love-in.

For the first time since we were lined up and he shrugged on the cloak, Kotah smiles.

That's it, Wolf.

We've got this.

Kotah

The influx of love feeds my soul and I remind myself of what matters. My mates are here. I can be the change I need to see in the Fae Realms, and as soon as we're done with this ceremony, it's nothing but Jaxx's latest drinking game, chicken nachos, and getting naked with my mates.

Calli's right. I can play the part for a couple of hours.

With them at my side, I can endure anything.

As the officiant drones on about my father's legacy and lists off all his contributions to the world we live in today, I stare at the wooden replica of his likeness and realize that stiff, wooden, and inanimate suits him.

That's a terrible thing to think, but it's true.

He doesn't hold the power to control me anymore.

He can't hurt me.

So, when the coronation minister hands me the torch, I touch the thirsty twigs of the pyre and don't mourn the man.

I mourn what I never got from him. I mourn the fact that what was wrong between us will never be put right. I mourn for the pain my sister feels over the loss of her father.

But I don't mourn him.

After circling the pyre once with the symbolic flame meant to release him from his earthbound duties, I reclaim my place at the front of the auditorium and watch the flames burn. I'm not sure if I thought it would change anything or not.

It doesn't.

The part of me that should ring in with anguished thoughts and emotions about losing the head of my family shut down long ago.

As the flames roar in the foreground, and the Coronation Minister drones on about duty and the exciting days before us, I glance to where my mother and Keyla sit.

Mother is perched on the front of her seat, her back as straight as an iron rod, her chin raised, her jaw clenched. She is the image of self-contained, emotionless strength.

As usual.

Keyla is holding up well. I know and respect that she had a different relationship with Father. She's hurting and mourning a man I didn't know.

I both pity and envy her that.

Our gazes meet and I offer her a smile.

True to Keyla's nature, she presses her index finger to her thumb and makes the universal 'okay' hand signal. It's something she started when we were kids and our parents berated me for any number of perceived offenses. She'd stand silently on the sidelines and make that signal. I shift my hands clasped at my front and return the signal.

Yeah, I'm okay.

"—and as the wheel of the year dictates, the leaves have fallen and the reign of our beloved leader slips into the slumber of winter. We mourn the fact that he was taken too soon but take comfort in the knowledge that the new growth of spring is upon us. From the death and decay of winter comes the bloom of new leadership. Nakotah Northwood…."

I zone out thinking about the 'too soon' part of his comment. Adahy believes Raven was drugging Father and that's why he's dead. She saw her lacing his food with something and immediately afterward, she was cursed and lost her place as my weapons instructor.

Could Adahy be right?

Raven has always been solid support for both my parents. Keyla doesn't believe it's possible. I just don't know.

I close my eyes, focusing on the mating bond which is lit and glowing with the love of my mates.

I take a knee when Mother approaches with Father's laurel and try not to see the lack of faith in her gaze as she places it on my head. "May the reign of wildlings continue and the members of the fae rejoice in their new king. To my son, Nakotah, may you live long and rule as a Fae Prime of the people and for the people."

Mother's words ring in my ears and then it's done.

I stand, sweep the train of my cloak to the side, and turn to the gathered masses.

Despite my trepidation, the smile I offer the fae community is genuine. I love our people and will do my best to serve them well. The crowd stands as the drummers begin. It's done. I'm Fae Prime, king of the preternatural world on earth.

The roar of celebration is deafening but doesn't drown out the alarm going off on my mating bond. Connected as we are, I sense the moment the chain of love is broken by fear.

Both Brant and Hawk are looking at their FCO watch communicators. When they lift their heads, things flip into high alert.

"Gun!" Hawk launches and takes me to the ground.

CHAPTER FOUR

Calli

Brant tackles me at the same moment Hawk shouts and races toward Kotah. I don't hear what he yells over the noise of the crowd, but I feel his alarm and recognize the look on his face.

We're under attack.

It takes a moment for the danger to register to the masses but when the air explodes with the *tat-tat-tat* of semi-automatic gunfire the ceremony erupts into chaos.

"Let me up," I say, breathless under Brant's weight. When he hesitates, I push harder. "Bear, I'm bulletproof, remember? Let me shift and I'll be safer than flattened underneath you."

He grunts and rolls to the side, his bear weighing in on that with a growl as he shifts to his bear.

Freedom reclaimed. I kick off my shoes and launch into the air as my body explodes into flame. My phoenix ascends fast and with a fury.

Where are my mates?

I level off my flight, circle around, and hover over

the scene, searching for—there –Jaxx's jaguar and Brant's bear are racing through the crowd, weaving between panicked guests and heading for the men shooting indiscriminately to scatter innocent people.

With everyone wearing their finest for the coronation, it's easy to spot the offensive team dressed in black battle fatigues. It's thoughtful of them to wear a uniform.

The party crashers are moving in on Kotah.

With a shrill scream, I push forward and swoop the crowd. My coordination has become lethal good. I have no trouble plucking the attackers out of the crowd with my talons, squeezing them tight, and then dropping the crumpled men to grab the next ones.

When they realize they are getting picked off, the offensive team turns its weapons on me. That's fine. If they're wasting ammunition on the fiery phoenix there's less for them to spray through the crowd.

I draw their fire and continue to swoop, clutch, and toss. My phoenix is fueled with the power of retribution and though the balance of power between me and my wild side is a give and take, I admit I'm more than a little influenced by her lust for vengeance.

Gunfire rings off behind me and I arc back around to check on my mates once again. Kotah has gone wolf and is fighting with Doc and Keyla, ripping the throat out of the man closing in on his sister and mother.

Hawk is moving with Lukas to secure the members of the Fae Council pinned and being picked off. I launch forward and move in to help them. The Fae Council might not be trustworthy or even my favorite people, but next to the Fae Prime, they are the most important members of the realm.

I'm locked on and descending when I recognize a face in the opposing team. Mischief, Sonny's Sergeant at Arms in the Sovereign Sons, is here and he's moving in on Hawk's back.

Bile builds at the base of my throat as the memory of his hold on me rages forward. I feel the pain of his pointy fangs clamping closed over my collarbone and smell the stench of his breath flooding my sinuses as he drew his hot, wet tongue up my cheek.

I land on the ground between him and Hawk and hold my wings out to screen his view.

"Barbie, I was hoping we'd meet again." His words don't affect me half as much as the lust lacing his tone. How did he slip through the cracks? He must not have been at the Sovereign Son's compound when we took out Sonny and his men.

Well, he won't escape his funeral twice.

I launch twenty feet in the air and swoop at him. My approach is aggressive, and I extend my talons. The razor-sharp tips are extended. We're not going for a grab and squeeze this time. We're going in for the kill.

Right before I get him in my grasp, he throws his arm out and hits me with an icy fireball.

The magical projectile explodes against my skin and frizzles and fritzes out my heat. Stupid drow assholes. I land in an uncontrolled run, stumbling into him and knocking us both to the ground in a tangle of limbs. My skin is molten and I'm not human.

Still, in my fiery female form, I fight him on the ground and grip his throat. His eyes flare wide. The smell of burning flesh is sweet revenge.

"You should've stayed under your rock, Mischief."

His eyes roll back and then power explodes off him like a sonic wave. Wind whistles in my ears as I'm thrown back. I hit a row of seating and crash to the grassy ground buried beneath a pile of folding chairs.

He stomps at me and I roll to my feet.

Part of me is glad he didn't die easily. There's still so much I want him to suffer for. The other part of me wants to be done with him so I can focus on my mates.

Before I debate which option I want more, Mischief raises his palm and throws a pulse of energy at me. I dive to the side and roll back to my feet unharmed.

Straightening, I hold my wings out to shield his view from the rest of the battle. My wingspan isn't as impressive in this form, but it's still impressive. "I'm not the same woman you bullied and beat on a few months ago, asshole. You won't be hopping on your bike and riding away from this one."

"If you say so. Personally, I like my odds."

I chuckle, focus on the fire inside me, relinquish my hold, and let my phoenix ascend fully. My firebird reignites and more than doubles my size. Towering over my old tormentor, I tilt my beak back and scream.

As I stomp over the chairs in my way, Mischief stumbles back, the fear in his eyes so damned rewarding.

Hawk

Lukas and I pick off another half a dozen men as we secure the members of the Fae Council. We haven't saved them all. There are at least two down with fatal wounds and another two not looking good. As we move in, the scent of dark magic singes my nostrils. I rub my nose and frown. "Is that you?"

Lukas ejects his empty magazine and reloads. "Are you implying I stink like rotten magic?"

"Just a question, sunshine. Don't get defensive."

Lukas grunts. "Nope. Not me."

"Then who's here that we don't know about?"

I barely have the words out of my mouth when a pulse of energy brings the hair on my arms up on end. Twisting, I raise my gun and search for the source of the disruption. "A portal's opening. Where is it?"

Lukas and I close ranks, standing back to back as the air on the other side of the auditorium lights up with an electrical field. "Fuck. Kotah's right there."

I launch into a full-out run, not knowing who or what will come out from the other side of that portal. All I know is no one will take Kotah from us. Whether this is about stopping the Fae Prime from taking power or the Phoenix Quint from uniting the realms, my mates are off-limits.

I'm fifty feet from Kotah and Keyla when an eight-foot-tall greater fae steps through the energy-charged air. Shrouded by shadow on a bright and crisp autumn afternoon, I fight to see through the illusion of his glamor.

The massive rack of antlers rising from his head and the massive horn hanging from his neck send a shiver down my spine. The maze of antlers points in every direction and reach more than four feet. They are speared with dagger-sharp points so he can drop to all four and become a beast in battle at a moment's notice.

"The Forest Lord," Lukas says.

"Fuck. I was hoping we'd seen the last of him."

Lukas and I push harder, but no matter how hard our legs pump, there's no getting there in time.

"Kotah!"

Kotah turns, grabs his sister, and throws them both bodily out of the beast's path. Calli's squawk of rage means she sees it too. A fiery wall of flames shoots from the sky, dividing the massive monster from Kotah and his sister.

For a moment, I breathe a sigh of relief… and then I read the telegraphing of his gaze. Turning back to where Kotah and Keyla had been standing a moment ago, the Forest Lord changes targets and grabs Raven and Kotah's mother.

A split-second later, they're gone.

"Well, fuck."

Jaxx

"Is everyone alright?" Most of the crowd has scattered by the time I get back to where my parents are helping people regroup. It looks like most injuries are scrapes and bruises, but others won't see tomorrow.

"We're fine, son," Daddy says, straightening. He's taken off his shirt and has torn it into strips to be used to tie off wounds. "Tend to your guardian duties. Your mother and I aren't going anywhere."

I kiss Mama's cheek and continue over to where Doc and Hawk are trying to calm Keyla. She's a wreck and my heart drops. "What happened? Where's Kotah?"

Hawk straightens and grabs my arm. "He's fine. It's not him. The Prima was taken."

"What? Why?"

"That's yet to be determined, but our boy is fine. He's right there with Calli and Brant."

I peel off and bolt to the side of the raised dais not slowing down until I'm chest to chest with my wolf. Breathing deep, I take his scent to the bottom of my lungs.

"Are you alright? Dammit… I was so scared when I saw Keyla crying."

Kotah's arms come around me and his hold grounds me enough to stop my cat from breaking free and going on a clawing rampage. "Jaxx… you're crushing me."

"Shit. Sorry." I ease off the rib-cracking hug and ease back. I'm trembling and I shake out my hands trying to shed the panic. "I love you, Wolf."

He palms my jaw and smiles. "You're the one who's good in a crisis, remember. I'm fine. I'm whole. And I'm right here with you. Calm down."

I swallow and let that sink in. "Good. Okay, I'm good. Just lost my shit there for a minute, but I'm back to being a cool cat once again."

Calli chuckles and hugs me. "Glad you're whole too, puss. I saw your cat securing the guests. Your jaguar is badass and super sexy."

It dawns on me then that Calli's wearing Kotah's ceremonial fur robe. "Why isn't this burning off?"

Her grin splits wide, filled with delight. "I went from phoenix to woman aflame back to phoenix and then human. I think I've finally got a handle on my transitions."

"And with that, a handle on regulating your body temperature afterward?"

"Let's not jinx it, but maybe. I still can't manifest clothes, but I can cover up with whatever's lying around."

I laugh. "Whatever's lying around… like the royal ceremonial robe of the wildling wolves?"

Calli shrugs. "Yeah, just something I threw on."

I take another deep, steadying breath and exhale. "Okay, I'm good. Back to the problem at hand. Do we know what this was about? Why'd they take your mother and Raven?"

"I think I was the first target," Kotah says, "but Calli ended that with a wall of flame and a dive-bomb offensive."

"Nicely done, kitten. So then the Forest Lord changed his mind and took the Prima and her right-hand female?"

"Not just them," Lukas says, joining us. The ex-military warrior looks a little torn up and wind-blown, but other than a few scuffs and scrapes, unscathed. "Three members of the council were taken too."

"Do we think this was Hawk's father and his Black Knight minions?"

Lukas shrugs. "We can't say yet, but who else?"

"Mischief was here from Sonny's gang. If the Sovereign Sons were part of the Black Knight's illegal money-making operation, it makes sense that he'd be with them. He lost his entire club when we took them down."

Kotah frowns. "I thought the FCO got everyone in that gang during their raids."

"One slimeball dripped through the cracks."

"Are you okay, kitten?" I ask.

She lifts her chin and smiles. "My phoenix stomped him out of my life for good."

I've seen her phoenix stomp and the guy didn't have a chance. Too bad. Not sad. "So, do we think the people taken were targeted because they were in league with the Black Knight or his opposition?"

Kotah frowns. "I hate to speak ill of my mother, especially when she's been kidnapped and can't defend herself, but I would be more apt to believe she's in league with them."

"I'm sorry, Wolf." I squeeze his shoulder and send him as much reassurance as I can. "We'll figure it out and do our best to get her back quickly, I promise."

"Okay," Lukas says, eyeing the crowd and security scurrying around us. "I hate to tell you guys what to do, but with a portalling Forest Lord in the mix, I'd rather see you head inside for this chat session."

I nod. "Yeah, probably a good call. Thanks, man."

"Was it you who sent the alarm to Hawk and Brant?" Calli asks.

Lukas nods. "I was patrolling the palace grounds for the ceremony when one of my wards picked up an incoming force. I warded the auditorium to notify me if an influx of metal crossed the boundaries."

"You warded for bullets?" Calli says. "Clever boy."

He shrugs. "When that lit up, I hauled ass back here and sent Brant and Hawk the message on their personal devices. I figured no one would have their phones in the middle of the ceremony and that was the fastest way to warn you."

Calli hugs him, ignoring the fact that the guy goes all stiff and awkward. "You saved our butts once again."

"You're awesome, my man."

Kotah shakes his hand and then we head inside where it's—I'm not sure 'safer' qualifies—but safe from a portal shifting Forest Lord anyway.

Brant

Jaxx and Doc take Calli, Kotah, and Keyla inside the palace, and I join Hawk and Lukas on cleanup. I want to avail myself and try to figure out what exactly went down. "Was this about Kotah, or the Prima, or the Fae Council, or stirring up shit?"

Hawk scowls at the carnage and scratches at the back of his neck. "No idea. Let's see what we can find out. Lukas, I want the casualties from the attacking force identified ASAP. Find out who they are, where they were from, what species, and what their alignment was."

"And from there?"

"Move to the Fae Council dead, and then guests." Hawk scowls at the scene and sighs. "If my father is recruiting militia, it would help if we knew from where and what he's promising them. And if it's not him—and that's a big if—knowing that will help us figure out who we're dealing with."

"On it. Stay tight."

"Always. And thanks for the heads-up."

"Always."

Lukas jogs off and leaves the two of us to take on the task of questioning the Fae Council. "How hostile toward you do you think they are right now?"

Hawk arches a brow. "Let's see, I called them out to the entire realm and questioned their allegiance, I shut down their positions and took their jobs from them, and now I'm going to interrogate them about colluding with fae terrorism. I can honestly say I'm not expecting any Yule gifts this year."

I chuckle. "As a male intimately familiar with pissing people off, maybe I can be of assistance. How about you let me take the lead and you stand there looking autocratic and deeply upset by the entire event."

He frowns and leans close enough that I can smell the expensive cologne he wears. "I *am* autocratic and deeply upset by the entire event."

"Perfect, then you should be able to pull it off."

Hawk chuckles and falls in behind me. The fact that he's giving me the lead is a small miracle. Two weeks ago, we would've been at each other's throats pushing buttons and butting heads.

It's crazy what a no-holds-barred night of BDSM and rough sex can do to recalibrate the way you look at someone. Yeah, he's a tough, alpha ass, but he's so much more.

Hey, he's our tough, alpha ass, so there's that, too.

The members of the Fae Council are clustered together in the dignitary's box to the side of the raised dais.

I head straight to the Feline Prime, Dane. He's a wildling and, as such, I understand his senses best of all of them. The broad-shouldered male possesses the keen gaze of a hunter and a full mane of tawny hair.

"Minister," I say, holding out my hand. "Brantley Robbins, we met a couple of months ago regarding us being the Guardians of the Phoenix."

The lion nods. "I remember. You're Jaxx's mates. His Alpha Prime informs me that the quint is fully mated and from what we saw of your phoenix just now, Calliope has come into her powers."

Until I know who's side he's on, I'm not sharing anything he could use against us. "She's a remarkable female. We're very proud of her progress."

He glances past me and sends Hawk an icy glare. If looks could kill, Hawk would be circling the drain. "Barron."

"Minister," Hawk says. "It's been a tough day. I'm sorry to hear Pranton and Elange succumbed to their injuries."

"I'm surprised you feel that way… considering."

I give Hawk credit, he doesn't engage. "The important thing here, Dane, is figuring out what happened and why."

"Isn't that obvious? Someone didn't think your wolf pup should rise to the fore and take control of the realm."

My bear growls unbidden and I fight to hold back my mate instincts. "You may address him as the Fae Prime, His Majesty, or Nakotah Northwood. Call him a wolf pup again and there will be more bloodshed on this lawn today."

Dane arches a flaxen brow and it's a look I've gotten many times from Hawk. Is that an alpha thing? Too bad for him. He's not *my* alpha.

"Back to the point of the conversation," I say, circling back. "If the Black Knight wanted you all dead, there you were, eleven fae leaders, sitting neatly in a box. Instead, two are dead, a couple more of you injured, and three more taken. What do you think that means?"

"I can't comment on the workings of a demented mind."

I grin. "No. Of course not. I'm sure you're as clueless as you seem. If you think of anything, be sure to let us know."

CHAPTER FIVE

Jaxx

I usher everyone back inside the palace even though a million palace minions are running around. Doc and I have to work to shield the group and get them upstairs to our wing without incident. Doc takes Keyla into his suite to see if he can get her to calm down and rest. Daddy and Mama head to their suite to call Laney and let her know we're all fine. I take Kotah and Calli into our suite to regroup.

"First things first," I say, escorting them toward the stairs. "Let's get you out of this stupid coronation persona and back to my wolf."

"Yes please," Kotah says taking off the bejeweled platinum laurel and tossing it onto the couch as we pass by. "This makeup itches."

Calli shrugs off the wolf pelt vest and jogs up the stairs naked in front of us. "Man, that train is heavy. I feel a hundred pounds lighter now."

I watch the waggle of her bare ass as she climbs the stairs and smile. "Then I'm glad you're free of it, kitten."

Kotah flashes me a lascivious grin. "Me too."

Calli proceeds to the bedroom oblivious to us being horny males soaking up the view of her body and slips back in her comfy outfit from earlier.

I lead Kotah into the washroom and run the faucet. "How do you even get paint like this off your face without ruining the towels?"

Calli giggles as she opens the drawer of her makeup vanity and passes us a package of wipes. "I swear you're the most domesticated male I've ever met."

Now it's my turn to laugh. "Why, because I don't want to have to get the stains out of the towels?"

"Uh… yeah. How many alpha males do you know that worry about laundry stains?"

I pull a roll of paper towel out from the vanity and set myself up a little cleaning station. "I am completely secure with my manhood."

"As you should be," Kotah says, ripping a few squares off Calli's makeup remover wipes and swiping at his face. "Speaking of your manhood…"

"Hello? Yes? What about it?" My attention shifts and damn if I don't start to stiffen at the prospect that we might be getting up to something sexy.

Kotah tosses the gunked up wipes and then hangs over the sink going the soap and water route. "Have you got any ideas narrowed down for our after-party nacho night?"

With him busy with his face in the sink, I look over at Calli. She looks as surprised as I am. "Oh, I figured we'd probably put that celebration on hold. You know, until we figure out what Hawk's father is up to and have a plan to find your mother and the others?"

Straightening, he tugs off a few swatches of paper towel and dries off. When he lowers his hands, I'm relieved to see my mate's face staring back at me once again. I'd be even happier if he didn't look like I just kicked him in the groin. "Yes, you're probably right. We should stay focused."

Calli rushes in and helps him get the last bits of color off his hairline and under his ears. "Speak your truth, sweet prince. Don't shut down on us now. You get a voice in this mating. We always want to hear your thoughts."

"Yeah, always, buddy."

He looks from her to me and frowns. "It might sound selfish, but I don't want to wait until everything is worked out. With us, everything is never worked out. The promise of a mating fun night is what got me through today. I'm disappointed you don't want to continue with our plans."

"Oh, no one said we don't want to continue with our plans, sugar. I think all Jaxx was saying was that maybe the priorities shifted."

I step behind him to untie the leather thong holding his hair captive. Pulling the binding free, I undo the intricate plaiting Keyla so painstakingly wove together. Fingering through the lengths, I shake it out and let it hang loose to his very tight and fine ass.

"How about this? We'll see what Hawk and Brant come up with, we'll talk to Lukas about what he and his team found out over the past couple of days, and then we'll revisit. If we're all here and there's nothing to be done until tomorrow, we'll make the most of our night, 'kay?"

The dip in his chin is forced and stiff. "Of course."

My cat snarls within me and I curse. "Okay, no. You are a terrible liar and there's no way I'm bursting your balloon. If you need the night of play we planned, you get it. End of discussion. We'll make good use of the next few hours and then shut out the world. Naked nachos as planned."

"Crisis permitting," Calli adds. "You never can tell. The palace could explode around us and ruin our plans."

"True story." I wrap an arm around Kotah's back and kiss his freshly scrubbed cheek. "And, until then, how about Calli and I get you out of these clothes and consummate your kingship by giving you some royal treatment?"

Kotah's smile sets my cat back on an even keel. "Oh, yes, please. That's the only kind of royal treatment I enjoy."

Calli

Poor Jaxx. He truly is the passion of our group and is always trying to balance everyone's needs, which—by the look on Kotah's face—includes some extra love and support today. That's fine. It's no hardship to be needed by Kotah. And yeah, if his soul needs a little soothing, it's the least we can do to comply. He soothes our souls on the daily.

Reaching for the metal fasteners on the leather jacket he's wearing, I get things started. "Anything particular on your mind, sweetie?"

He shakes his head. "No. Simply to be lost in

pleasure for a while."

"Done deal," Jaxx says, the jaguar already naked and sporting one helluva stiff cock.

When all the fasteners are unlatched on his jacket, I slide my hands under the leather and shuck it off his shoulders. It plops to the tile floor and I drop my hands to his waist.

Jaxx shifts in behind him and rucks his shirt up to his chiseled abs and over his head. "I love that you went commando today, Wolf. A little bit of our sweet prince rebel even when forced to comply."

I chuckle at the flush in his cheeks and work the tie of his pants loose to open things up. "Little do they know."

Jaxx chuckles and grinds up behind him. "They don't get to know. You're ours, Nakotah Northwood. They don't deserve to know the real you."

My attention drops to the two naked men in front of me and I sigh. "I have entirely too much clothing on."

"Yes, you do, kitten. Let us help you with that."

I close my eyes as they shift closer, their hands caressing my thighs, my breasts, my ribs as they tunnel beneath my jeans and sweater to strip me down and join them in their naked glory.

I leave my eyes closed and soak in the sensations of fingers, lips, tongues, and the brush of their bodies against mine as they stroke and seduce.

"How about we move this somewhere more comfortable?" Jaxx says.

The world tilts as my legs are swept out from under me and I'm being carried out and toward the bedrooms.

When we don't head straight into the master but turn right and continue along the balcony, I open my eyes. "What have you got in mind, puss?"

His sexy smile is sin incarnate as he crosses the threshold to the kink room at the end. "I may have overheard you mention you and Kotah want your turns in the Den of Debauchery. I thought we can get some playtime logged in until Hawk feels more secure. Who knows, maybe he'll even join us and see there's nothing to worry about."

I'm about to respond when he tosses me into the air, and I bounce and skid naked across the mattress. "Hey, be nice."

Jaxx shakes his head. "Oh, no, kitten. This room isn't about being nice. If that's what you think then yeah, you do need some educating on what to expect."

My breath comes fast, and a rush of moisture hits me between the thighs. "What are you suggesting?"

Jaxx casts a glance at our wolf and smiles. "You good with a play session, wolf? I promise it'll take your mind off things and will end well for everyone."

Kotah nods. "Sounds good to me. What do you want me to do?"

Jaxx waggles his brow and purrs. "That depends on if you want to be the one tied down and trussed up or the one doing the tying? Your choice."

He worries his lip between his teeth and then smiles. "I want to be tied and trussed."

"Done. Come with me. Calli, we'll need the ankle and wrist cuffs. That cabinet, center drawer."

I hustle to the cabinet Jaxx pointed to and grab the

four padded cuffs. I meet the boys over by the tall 'X' in the middle of the room and offer up what I brought.

Jaxx picks two and leaves two for me. "Like this, kitten." He wraps Kotah's wrist and buckles the cuff closed. "They're very padded and cushy, so tight isn't a bad thing. Trust me."

I groan. "When do we get to see what you and Hawk get up to in here?"

Jaxx shrugs and moves up to Kotah's other wrist. "That's up to Hawk. He's come a long way but give him time. He's working through a lot to open up to the life we're promising him. He's trying and he's juggling a lot of other stuff at the same time."

I drop my attention to Kotah's ankle and sigh. "I know. I'll try. It's just so hot. I want to be part of it with you guys."

"For now, we'll start here." He offers me a hand to straighten when I finish Kotah's second ankle and then turns to our very amped up mate. "All set, my man?"

His grin is perfection, the strain of the day gone from his expression. "All set."

Kotah

The anticipation of what's coming is madness. Ever since I ordered the furniture, toys, and tools for this room I've been imagining what it would be like to have a kink session in here with my mates. Yes, Hawk is the most experienced, but I have no doubt Jaxx will make this a memorable event.

"Step back and let's get you locked in." Jaxx raises my wrist and locks the ring of the wrist cuffs into place.

Then he steps around to the other side and repeats the process.

Calli drops to the floor and follows his lead, lifting my foot, opening my leg, and latching the ankle cuff into place. When she does my second leg, I lean back against the steel and wood frame feeling more than a little exposed.

I wrap my fingers around the hand pegs and test the resistance. Yep, I'm well and truly restrained.

"Mmm, you make one sexy offering, Kotah. Doesn't he, kitten?"

"Stunning," she says, her gaze locked on my arousal standing tall against my abdomen. Having her stare at me so intently triggers a tingle in my balls and I pray I don't go off early and ruin this.

"Your cock's weeping for attention, Wolf," Calli says, closing her fingers around my length and giving me a couple of tugs. "You sure know how to make your girl happy."

Jaxx chuckles. "Now, kitten, don't get ahead of ourselves. We haven't even started playing yet."

"But I want to suck on my wolf."

"How badly?"

She bites on her bottom lip. "I ache for it."

When she looks at me like that, I do too.

Jaxx sees my hunger and wags his finger in the air. "Oh, no. It's not that easy, Wolf. In the master bedroom, we're all about instant gratification. The Den of Debauchery is about pushing limits and taking things to another level. Calli, you are free to run your hands over him, bite his sweet ass, tweak his nipples, and toy with his junk, but it's just playing for now."

I swallow, unsure how much I'm going to like kink. With Calli running her hands up the inside of my thighs and raking me with her nails while looking like she wants to devour me, instant gratification seems much more enticing.

Jaxx comes back, rolling a little table with lube, massage oils, vibrators, masks, and other toys I'm not sure of.

"Here, Wolf. Let me show you what fun we can have." He steps behind me and slides a blindfold over my eyes. The straps fasten with Velcro so an instant later, my visual senses are cut off.

My wolf growls.

"Are you okay, my man?"

I swallow and push back my survival instincts as they rush to the fore. "Yes."

"Safeword?"

"Hydrogen."

"Good man." He presses a warm hand against the side of my neck and my racing pulse pushes against his palm. "Trust me, Kotah. I've got you."

I draw a deep breath and relax into his touch. "I know you do. Sorry."

"Don't be sorry. We'll play a bit. If this doesn't fit your mood, say the word and we'll change tacks."

I shake that off. "No, I want to try. I've wondered and thought about it a lot. I'll be fine."

Calli

I meet Jaxx's gaze and I'm getting the same skepticism off him that I'm picking up on our mating bond. Kotah's not fine. I don't know if his day is catching up to him or it's the kink itself, but he's fronting.

I gesture to him and Jaxx frowns, nodding that he's picking up on it too. "Okay, kitten, work your magic on our wolf. Let's show him how special he is."

Jaxx abandons all the toys and when I move in on Kotah's front, he presses in from behind. "We love you, Kotah."

I run my hands down his thighs and for the first time ever, I see that Kotah is losing his erection. "Okay, no. I'm calling this over." I bend down to unbuckle his ankles.

Jaxx sees my point of concern and reaches up and unbuckles his wrists. "Yep, if it's not working for you, Kotah, it's not happening. Come here and let's have some mate fun."

We get him uncuffed and Jaxx takes his blindfold off and the three of us make our way over to the king-sized bed. Jaxx lays Kotah down and crawls in beside him, wrapping him in a full-bodied hug.

"I'm sorry, Jaxx," Kotah says, his voice thick with emotion. "I wanted to be good at this."

The tears in Kotah's voice have both Jaxx and I blinking fast. Jaxx growls. His cat usually makes happy, sexy noises, but this is not that. "Don't do that, Kotah. You're great and sexy as fuck and the most playful, giving lover we could ask for. It's totally fine and it makes sense that something like this might not turn your crank, buddy."

"Why do you say that?"

"Because you're an Omega. You get your strength from touch and feeding off the emotions of others. Restraints and delayed gratification might not be your thing. Your heart and soul are made for connection and feeling the emotion behind things. Don't give it another thought. Seriously. I should've thought of that before I brought you in here."

"But we're in a normal bed now," I say, running my hands across the sculpted planes of his abs. "There's plenty of connection now. And you can feel and touch and play without restriction."

I take his hand and slide it between the folds of my core. "Feel how wet I am for you, sweet prince?"

He closes his eyes and I wriggle a little, grinding into his touch. We both groan. I crawl closer, swing my knee over his hip, and prop myself over his chest.

Kotah responds to the sway of my breasts like I hoped he would. His eyes widen as they hang loose over his chest and just like that, we've got him back and the tension in him is easing.

"May I?" Jaxx asks behind me. He takes hold of Kotah's cock and our wolf's hips buck beneath me. A couple of strokes later and our jaguar is propping the full, warm tip of Kotah's erection at the entrance of my pussy.

"Sit back and ride him home, kitten."

I do. I push back, his solid length gliding inside me in slow, luscious inches. I rock over him a few times until he's fully inside me and I sit on the cradle of his hips.

Everything falls back into place.

Kotah's wanton smile is back as he tweaks my nipples, his cock is thick and hard, rubbing my insides in all the most delicious ways, and our mating bond is clear and vibrating with nothing but love.

"Rub my clit, wolf, please. I'm ramping up fast and I need you to touch me."

One of the best things about Kotah in bed is how dedicated he is to the needs of his partners. He holds his hand out to the side for a moment and Jaxx sets him up with a squirt of lube. When he slides his thumb between our bellies, the glide is not only slick but cool against my heated flesh. Tilting forward, I grip his shoulders and grind down.

"Oh, yes… You feel amazing inside me."

The world spins as he rolls us over and takes control. With me on my back beneath him, he thrusts deep, opening my legs wider. I lift my knees and give him all the access he needs.

"Watching him fuck you is sexy as hell, kitten." Jaxx's voice is husky, and the moist *click, click, click* of him tossing with a wet cock provides the soundtrack for our background noises.

"His long, mane of hair falling forward, brushing over the soft rounds of your tits. I know that feeling. It's like silk seduction."

It is. That's exactly what it feels like. And with every thrust and retreat, that silk drape tickles and teases my flesh. Tension tightens deep inside me and my orgasm builds.

"And then there's the view. Fuck, Kotah, your

muscles are so tight and toned beneath that beautiful copper skin of your heritage. Your body so supple and ready for the taking."

That's true too. Kotah's a beautifully made male. All tight lines and chiseled musculature beneath the velvet skin of a noble prince.

"Run your hands over his shoulders and down to his ass. Grab that ass, Calli, both hands. Yeah, dig your nails into the fleshy globes and pull him inside deeper."

I do as I'm told and Kotah grunts, his eyes wild with approval. "You like that wolf?"

"I do," he gasps, his breath coming out in bursts as the pumping gets wild and the two of us are rocking behind the force of his pounding thrusts. "Grip harder. Don't be afraid to hurt me."

I tighten my grip, knowing I'm probably breaking skin, but he's so hot for it. Gawd, I know the need for that sensation of pleasure-pain. And judging by the sweat beading on his forehead and the catch in his breath, he's not suffering.

His hunger triggers a keening of sensation in my clit, and my insides start to convulse. His cock feels so thick and long and is hitting me in all the right spots.

"Yes, sugar," I gasp, arching my back off the mattress. My orgasm detonates and my insides grab hold of his cock and milk the satin skin sliding over steel. I grip the sheets in my hands and let the sensation shatter me. "Don't stop."

"I'll never stop, *Chigua*."

The breathless reverence of his voice follows me as I retreat into the passionate waves of my orgasm as it crests and recedes. So good. So freaking good.

I'm still catching my breath when Jaxx rises on his knees behind Kotah. "Mind if I join in? You waggling your fine ass in the air is more than I can take and look, I made this special creamy lube just for you."

Kotah's smile is pure, sexy joy. "Ready and waiting, mate. My sexy ass is yours to claim whenever you want."

"Great answer." Jaxx's cum-filled hand disappears behind the round of Kotah's very fine backside and they both groan. Kotah's eyes roll closed as he pushes back against Jaxx's ministration and I'm cranking up again.

"This is what I want, wolf. I want to finger you until I can fuck you hard and then I'll mark you as mine. Again. And maybe again and again."

Kotah's jaw flexes as he swallows. "I want that too."

Jaxx's golden bicep flexes as he works to prime Kotah and gets him stretched for what's to come. "How does that feel my king?"

"So good."

Jaxx works him over a little longer and then positions himself behind Kotah. The lube bottle gives off a little squelch and then Jaxx is squaring up and penetrating him.

It can take a few minutes to relax the muscles enough to get rocking with anal, so I spend the time sticking my tongue in his mouth and winding myself up again for round two. A few minutes later, Jaxx presses inside Kotah as Kotah presses inside me.

I stretch and close my eyes, soaking up the rock and

thrust of Jaxx fucking us both.

"Life is good."

CHAPTER SIX

Hawk

Brant and I finish speaking with the members of the Fae Council and help palace security with the aftermath of the attack. It feels like ages before we're done and back at our suite. When we get inside and lock the door, all the angst and turmoil of the past two hours is set aside.

"Hey, mates." Jaxx meets us at the door with a hug. "Another attack and we're all still standing."

Brant claps him on the back and then looks around. "Where are Calli and Kotah?"

"In the master snuggled up with snacks and watching Princess Bride."

"Again? Inconceivable." Brant takes off his boots and points to the cheese and meat tray on the kitchen island. "Is this going up?"

"Yeah, thanks. Go ahead. We'll be right up."

I make an event of unlacing my dress shoes and once Brant is upstairs and in the bedroom, I straighten and ease in. "What's wrong?"

Jaxx leads me through the living room and into the

office. The fact that we need distance and privacy puts me on edge. By the time we get to where we're going, my pulse is pumping hard.

Jaxx sees my alarm and raises his palms. "It's fine now, but I think we need to be extra sensitive around Kotah for a while."

"Is he still raw because of the ceremony and his mother?"

"No. Nothing like that. He wanted us to take his mind off things and forget for a while, so I took him into the Den."

Shit. The look on Jaxx's face makes me afraid to ask. "And what went wrong?"

"He froze up and shut down."

I've played in the lifestyle long and hard enough to know that it absolutely happens, but damn, I wish I'd been here for him. "How badly?"

"Not bad. We hadn't even gotten started really. Calli and I blindfolded him, cuffed him, and locked him onto the cross, and that was it. His wolf ascended and his cock softened."

"How'd you end it?"

"We got him unhooked fast, took him onto the bed, and had a normal, love-in session."

"And that went okay? Brant and I felt the connection of the three of you, so you were able to bring him back around?"

He nods. "That went great. Super successful like always. I just think he's in his head now… like maybe he thinks he won't be enough for us in the future."

I curse and exhale. "When you say *us*… you mean

me. Fuck. This is what I was afraid of. Okay, well, it was bound to happen because he and Calli have both been pushing, so we'll deal with it. I'll spend extra time showing him how perfect he is being his sexy and sweet self."

Jaxx nods. "You've been hesitant with Calli too. Do you think she'll have trouble?"

"Yeah, I do. She was stalked by her uncle, and then pinned and almost raped and beaten by the trucker, the drow, and gods only know how many others over a decade on the streets. I honestly think restraint and dominance is the last thing she needs. Her subconscious mind has locked shit down and built up walls for a reason. I say we don't fuck with it."

"She thinks she wants more."

"I read people for a living and have been in the lifestyle for my entire adult life. No matter what she thinks, she doesn't want what we do."

"So how do you want to handle it?"

I cast a glance past Jaxx and ensure there are no prying ears. "With Kotah, we relish the love. With Calli, when she wants to be naughty, we take her in for some light play. I honestly don't believe she'll enjoy the dominance and power exchange that you and Brant do."

Jaxx nods. "Agreed, so we keep it kink lite unless it's the two of us or Brant."

I nod. "And we keep the full details of our sessions really fucking private."

"Agreed." Jaxx closes the distance and hugs me.

The tension in Jaxx's frame is unwelcome. I don't doubt that Kotah freezing up on him, affected him deeply. Easing back, I grasp his jaw and lay a long, hot kiss on those lips I love so much. "This is *not* your fault. It happens. We'll fix it like we fix everything—together."

Jaxx exhales a heavy breath and nods. "Yeah, okay."

I kiss him again for good measure and step back. "Now, let's get upstairs before Brant eats all the snacks."

Jaxx snorts. "Oh, I'm sure the ship has sailed on that one. I'll make more."

Calli

Jaxx and Hawk join us about ten minutes after Brant. I have no doubt our jaguar filled him in on what happened and the fact that Hawk beelines it straight for Kotah proves me right. "Shove over Bear," he says, climbing in from the foot of the bed and crawling up to join us.

Kotah stiffens and the tension and emotion from earlier resurfaces. When Hawk pulls him against his chest, Kotah's eyes are far too glassy for my liking. When the tears start, I'm curling in too.

"What's wrong?" Brant says, looking around. "What did I miss?'

"It's been a day," Jaxx says, bringing in more food. "Kotah's taken enough hits to warrant an emotional meltdown, don't you think?"

"Shit yeah. Today's been shit all the way around."

I snuggle into Brant and steal the last piece of kielbasa. "It's over now and we survive to fight another day. Go, team."

Kotah

Keyla, Doc, Mama, Daddy, and Lukas arrive at our suite at six for dinner and a planning session. One thing I've learned about the Stanton family… when a crisis hits, they cook. Which, with a family of wildlings, is a good thing. Adahy had already sent up all my favorite desserts to console me on a difficult day, so we're set to reset.

I'm still a little embarrassed by my reaction in the playroom and then falling apart when Hawk came in to join us, but true to my mates, they didn't seem to mind a bit. My father would've been horrified I crumbled and did it in front of others. I'm the Fae Prime and should be held to a standard of strength above all others.

But my father is dead.

I'm not him and I'm glad about that.

My mates love me and support me and though I still need to have 'the talk' with Hawk, for now, everything is alright, and we can fake it until we make it.

"Eat up, baby boy," Mama says, sliding another helping at me. "You need your strength for whatever comes next."

I smile and start in on the offering. It doesn't bother me that Mama calls me baby boy. She calls Jaxx that too. "Thank you, Mama."

She winks and moves on to topping up Brant's plate.

"What do we know for sure?" Hawk asks.

Lukas straightens in his stool at the island and swallows. "There are no crowd fatalities even though there were a lot of injuries due to the stampeding and several others caught by a ricochet. The only dead are the two members of the Fae Council and the only unaccounted for are three counselors—one being the Minister of the Council—the Prima, and Raven.

"Could it be..." Calli stops mid-sentence and waves the attention away. "Never mind."

"No, kitten," Jaxx says. "Brainstorming is an all-thoughts considered process."

Calli swallows and casts me an apologetic gaze. "Could it be the Black Knight—"

"—Daddy Dearest," Hawk adds.

"Yeah. Could it be that Mr. Whitehouse gathered his collaborators either to contain them or to keep them from being discovered and interrogated?"

Keyla puffs up and I raise a hand before she jumps down Calli's throat. "It's possible."

My sister pegs me with a hostile gaze and crosses her arms. "You don't honestly believe that, do you?"

"I'm not writing her off as the enemy, Keyla, but it's possible. Maybe Adahy is right and it's all Raven. Mother might've been caught in the crossfire. Maybe I wasn't supposed to take my oath today and Mother was going to step in. Maybe the Fae Council already had a plan in place if I was killed to put someone else into power who aligns with their objectives. We don't know."

Keyla swipes her fingers across her cheeks. "I know Mother would never agree to have you killed and I know she'd never stand with people who planned to do you harm."

"And you know her best, so we'll take that as truth."

Brant finishes his plate and collects Calli's and Jaxx's before taking them to the sink.

"Are we any closer in finding out if the counselors

who were taken were targeted because they were on board with the Black Knight or opposed?"

Cue the shaking heads.

"Hawk would have the greatest insight on the Minister of the Council," Calli says.

Hawk sends her a scowl. "What makes you say that?"

I expect Calli to point out that he is the only person in the room who had sex with her, but she surprises me. "You vetted and put together the Fae Council."

Hawk relaxes a little and gestures to Lukas. "We pulled the vetting files the moment doubt was cast on the council. Lukas cross-referenced them with bank records, social media comments, and political stances and found nothing definitive."

"The Minister did speak out against expanding the governing council," Daddy says.

"When was that?" Hawk asks.

"At the Monster Rights Conclave last month."

Hawk frowns. "What session?"

"You weren't there, son. It was after the panel spoke. A sprite in the audience asked about the recent protests and suggested that expanding representation to include some of the lesser fae races and diminutive classes might alleviate tensions."

"And the Minister was opposed?"

"Oh, she said all the appropriate things like 'the balance of representation is complex, and the council is always eager to consider ways of improving how they serve the people."

"But you felt it was lip-service?"

"Oh, it definitely was. I was sitting close enough to smell their annoyance at the suggestion and the lie when she outright said she'd take it to the council for consideration."

Brant growls. "Well, she's in for a rude awakening when we reunite the realms because there will be plenty of fae, of all power levels, who will need consideration. The power of eleven is ending. Who knows what the new Fae Council of the United Realms would look like?"

"Which goes to motive," Lukas says. "Stop the merging of the realms and keep their power without question."

"So, that implies that the counselors taken were with Hawk's father and the ones who were killed were against," Calli says.

"Question their spouses," Mama says. "As you five know, when your mate is facing opposition and upset, a spouse is often informed beyond what he or she is supposed to know."

Lukas nods. "Good thought, Maggie. I'll track them down as soon as we're done here."

"Why take Raven and Mother?" Keyla asks. "They can't influence the vote of the Fae Council, so why take them?"

Doc frowns. "I'm with Keyla on this. They have to know between the Guardians and the Fae Prime, you'll amass a force and track them down. Taking the Fae Prima put them on every watch list on the continent."

"I'm not sure they were the target," Hawk says. "The Forest Lord was zoned in on Kotah. It was only when Calli's firewall blocked him from getting to our wolf that he turned and went after the Prima and Raven."

Keyla frowns. "You're saying she might've been taken simply because his chance at grabbing Kotah and me was eliminated?"

"Yes," Hawk says. "It's a sleight of hand move like when he attacked us on the road to keep me from noticing he was kidnapping gifted kids and fucking with my company."

"Language, love," Mama says.

"Sorry, Maggie," Hawk blushes. "But you get my point. They came at us in a big, flashy event and took one of the most iconic members of our community and it plays perfectly into his plans."

"To distract us," Jaxx says. "He wants us to stop searching the old portal gate sites."

Hawk nods. "Yeah. And that means there's something to find or he wouldn't go to all the trouble."

I sigh and run my fingers over my face. "He sounds as manipulative and twisted in strategy as my father."

Hawk shrugs. "It's all part of making us who we are and getting us to this place, wolf. Now we get to use all those years of mental anguish to turn the tables and beat them at their own game."

"I like the sound of that."

Keyla doesn't look pleased about any of this. "That sounds like you're *not* going to amass a force and start looking for our Mother. So, what, you're going to carry on visiting old gate sights and ignore the Fae Prima's kidnapping?"

"Technically, Calli is the Fae Prima," Brant says.

Keyla frowns. "No. Technically, she's not."

"What do you mean?" Calli asks.

Keyla stares at me and frowns. "The coronation is over but you're not Fae Prime until you sign the declaration and it's registered downstairs. Mother was supposed to escort you there after the ceremony."

"Well, that's an important factoid you might've mentioned earlier," Brant snaps.

Jaxx stands. "Okay, first things first. Let's get the Prime stuff locked down and finalized. We didn't go through all this to be voided out at the last minute."

Jaxx

The procession down to the registry office might seem like overkill to anyone looking from the outside, but this is our family. The five of us, Mama and Daddy, Keyla and Doc, and Lukas. If my sister Laney was here, she'd be tromping down the stairs too.

And while we're here to offer moral support, we're also here to make sure no one tries to stop this from happening. As much as none of us likes the idea of Kotah being made a puppet in the politics of the realm, he's the rightful heir to the position, and at least with him in power, we know there's an honest and trustworthy leader at the helm.

When we get to the registrar's office, the door is locked.

"That's weird," Keyla says, knocking on the glass. "This office is open nine until nine."

When no one comes to let us in, Hawk steps aside and gestures for Lukas to try the door next.

Lukas tries the knob, presses his hand over the lock plate, and tries again. When the doorknob still doesn't give way, he frowns and starts waving his hands the way he does when he's doing mage spellwork.

I'm not sure why he'd need to go to so much effort to open a simple door but when he's finished, it opens without trouble. The ten of us file in and what do you know, the staff are in there and working like normal.

When we step inside, the sprite at the front desk looks up and I wonder if she might faint.

"Hey there," I say, "No one answerin' the door today?"

"I'm sorry, what?"

"The door was locked. We knocked and no one came to let us in. We're here to register Nakotah Northwood as the next Fae Prime. He's been waitin' in the hall."

"I… I'm so sorry. I didn't hear knocking."

"Okay, how about gettin' us hooked up? Have you got the Fae Prime registration papers ready?"

She blushes and her eyes bug wide. "I believe Counselor Pranton took the paperwork up for the ceremony."

"Spoiler alert," Brant says. "The ceremony didn't end well for Counselor Pranton. How about you print off a copy and we try again. We'll have to call a mulligan."

"Um... okay, give me one second. I'll get my manager." The girl jumps off the platform that raises her to serve people and rushes off. She returns a moment later with a well-dressed forest elf.

The male rushes in and at least looks the part of a

manager eager to help. "Your Highness, what an honor. I'm Neymar Grans, Chief Registrar. Plia explained and will run to the print room now and pick up the duplicates I requested. We'll have you registered and notarized in short order."

"Thank you, Chief Grans," Kotah says. "May I ask why the door was locked?"

He shakes his head. "I'm at a loss. I unlock it when I arrive in the morning and lock it again at night when I leave. I'm the only one here today with a key."

"It was locked with magic, not a key," Lukas says. "Who on your staff has that ability?"

He shrugs looking perplexed. "No one that I'm aware of. I'm sorry. I don't know anything about that."

"But you are aware of the recent efforts of the Black Knight to usurp control of the FCO and the Fae Council?" Hawk asks. "I assume you saw my public announcement?"

"Yes, sir. I think everyone has seen it."

"Good, because today's attack was another attempt to derail our society. I want this paperwork completed and recognized before we leave here. There will be no way to contest Nakotah once this is complete, is that correct?"

"No sir. He's the blood heir to the preceding Fae Prime. He was declared the Prime in Waiting and was crowned at his public coronation. The registry paperwork is all that is left.

"Here we are," Plia says, running in to join us. "Hot off the presses and ready to sign."

Neymar reaches across the counter and takes the

pages. With practiced efficiency, he counts the pages, checks that everything is in order, and turns the paperwork toward us. “A pen Your Majesty. I’ll turn the pages, and if you sign where I indicate, you’ll be all set.”

Kotah takes the pen and follows Neymar’s instructions. When he’s done, the elf turns the pages back to himself, goes through them once more, and then signs, dates, and stamps the registration papers. “And who will stand as the witnesses? It has to be someone not related by blood or family.”

“Lukas and Doc, you’re up,” I say.

The two of them shift forward and sign on the line.

When that’s done, Neymar pulls a purple-waxed candle out of a locked drawer in the counter, he lights the wick and lets it drip in the bottom corner. “Would you like to do the honors, Majesty?”

Kotah takes the seal, checks the image on the end, and presses it into the wax.

“Congratulations, Majesty. It’s an honor to be the one to announce that you are the new Fae Prime.”

Kotah forces a smile like the trooper he is. “Thank you for all your help.”

“And just in time too,” a pixie says, flying through the offices behind.

“What do you mean by that?” Hawk asks, waving her closer. “Why are we just in time?”

“Because there’s a negation clause in the laws of the coronation. If the Fae Prime registration paperwork isn’t filed on the same day as the coronation, it can be contested. In another forty-five minutes, we would’ve been closed for the night and you would’ve been chasing us down and scrambling."

Brant's bear lets off a murderous growl. "But we're good now, right?"

She nods. "Oh, yes. Everything's in order."

I shake my head. "Hawk, I'm really gettin' tired of your father interferin' in our lives."

Hawk chuffs. "Now multiply that by a million and you can imagine how I feel."

CHAPTER SEVEN

Hawk

I wake with a start and sit bolt upright in bed.

"What is it?" Kotah whispers beside me, his eyes wide. "One of your dreams?"

"No, I'm fine," I squeeze his arm and roll out of bed, grabbing Jaxx's flannel pants off the floor as I go. "Just an idea. Go back to sleep."

I'm out the door and halfway down the stairs when I realize he's right behind me. I pivot on the steps. "Really, wolf. You don't need to forfeit sleep for this. It's probably nothing."

He finishes pulling up his pajama bottoms and continues to close the distance. "I wasn't sleeping anyway. Maybe getting up and solving one of life's mysteries might help calm my wolf."

"Is he pacing? Are you alright?"

Kotah stops on the stair above me and meets me eye-to-eye. "It's not like when I was poisoned. He's just anxious. Do you ever feel like no matter how hard you try, life is happening *to* you instead of *around* you?"

"Only every day I lived with my father and every

day since he crawled out of the woodwork."

He nods. "That's how my wolf and I feel—like we need to do something instead of being steered and manipulated into reacting all the time."

"I call it the marionette malaise. The distress of always feeling like you're someone's puppet."

"Exactly."

I know how he feels all too well. "Okay, if you want to put on the kettle and warm up some of those cinnamon buns, I'll grab my laptop and meet you at the table. We can look through what my subconscious mind barfed up in my dreamland epiphany and then maybe we can feel more pro-active."

His smile, as always, leaves me warm inside. "Perfect."

I meet him back at the table a few moments later. He's got our sweet treats warmed and the kettle is hissing and almost ready to click off. "Did you want tea with these?"

"Hot chocolate and Baileys if you're game?"

"Coming right up."

I've got my laptop open and am calling up my files when he pulls the chair around to check out what I'm reading. "What's this?"

"Maybe nothing. When all this started, like in the early days when Calli resurrected, Jayne and I were working on fae land contracts and were arguing about a survey that didn't match our records. You see," I point to the two aerial surveys. "In the deed, the ownership of the land is divided by the river, so this is fae land on this side of the river and the land on this side is owned privately. But here, look. In the more recent survey."

"The river moved." Kotah frowns. "That can happen, can't it? With erosion and changing weather and flooding?"

"It can, but I sent my science team out there and they deemed it an unnatural occurrence. They say someone dammed and redirected the flow of the river until it diverted to where it flows now."

"Who and why?"

"I have no idea, but…" I pull out the file listing the locations of the dismantled portal gates, "it struck me that this might be where one of the old portal gate sites fell. Check out the location in the fire dervish forest. It's based on the description of where the river falls."

"So a decade ago it was there on the fae land and it might still be there… but by the survey maps, it would now be on the other side of the river and potentially hidden from people trying to find it and destroy it?"

"*Potentially* being the key word."

He stares at the fae land in the old survey and compares it to the newer one. "It's a big assumption, Hawk."

"But it's enough for us to take a closer look."

He nods. "Agreed. What I don't understand is why? Moving the river was done over a decade ago. Why?"

I pop the last bite of my cinnamon roll into my mouth and sit back in my chair. "What if someone knew what was on the horizon and acted to protect a gate to join the realms?"

Kotah looks skeptical. "That's a big leap. It's more likely a dishonest developer who wanted more land attributed to his property."

I lick the icing off my fingers and shrug. "Possibly, but I don't think so. My gut is telling me we're onto something and my gut's usually on the mark."

"I suppose someone with precognitive abilities could've seen what was coming and taken steps."

"And we've come to that conclusion more than once recently. That's our assumption about who Riley is and what happened there. Hell, maybe there's more intervention happening than we know about."

"I think there is a lot more to this than we know about."

"Exactly, so, let's check it out."

Kotah smiles. "Pennsylvania isn't far. If we leave in the morning, we can be there before lunch."

Kotah

My mind is awhirl. I hope Hawk is right, but honestly, at this moment, I don't care. What I love most about this plan is that it gets the five of us out of the palace and doing what we do best—figuring out the puzzles of our Guardian world.

For the next half hour, Hawk combs through the information that Jayne forwarded from the ecological people and cross-references it with the location listed about where the portal gates used to be found.

I find his dedication and focus admirable and quite sexy. To see him in his element as a big-picture power player is a gift. I finish another one of the cinnamon buns and push them away before I make myself sick.

"If we're heading out first thing, should we go back

to bed so we're not zombies?" I ask.

Hawk's amped up and while I appreciate how his mind sees complexities and different facets of reality, in this case, I worry he might be disappointed.

There are a lot of question marks in his logic.

Hawk leans forward and grips my cheeks sweeping his tongue into my mouth. He's happy and hopeful and surging with emotions I rarely get from contact with him. "Yeah, sure, we could go back and try to sleep... or, since we're both up... maybe we can both get it up and celebrate?"

Hawk arches a dark brow and my wolf prowls forward. As much as I like the idea... "Maybe we should get some sleep. It was a rough day yesterday. I'm not sure I'm up for much."

There's a pregnant pause while he seems to consider my answer. When he dips his chin and leans toward me, my heart starts rabbiting in my chest. His lips are scorching hot on mine, and his hands grip both sides of my neck as he kisses me. My wolf howls inside and I try to stay in the moment.

He's kissing me... and not like he's trying to cheer me up or reassure me. He's kissing me like he needs the connection. Which is perfect because I do too.

He shifts out of his chair and lifts me to my feet and suddenly, my mind is filled with every erotic image and position I can think of.

He could bend me forward against the table and take me from behind. He could lay me on the island and lift my knees. He could push me to my knees and grip my hair as he fucks my mouth. I'm leaking cum thinking about it.

He must smell my desperation because it's rife in the air between us. Another thing between us is my rock hard cock pressing at the fabric of my flannel pants.

There's no way he can miss it.

I'm practically spearing his abdomen.

And then I remember what happened with Jaxx earlier and my heart aches. I slow our kiss and step back. "I'm sorry. It's not you."

Hawk's gaze is hot and serious, his chiseled jaw clenched. "No. I think it is. Jaxx told me what happened."

The sting of my humiliation burns the rim of my eyes and I turn away. "I'm not giving up. I want to be like that—to share that kind of sex with you. I'll get there."

"Maybe, but honestly, I hope you don't."

I turn back and peg him with a glare. Heat flares in my chest and if my life-giving organ were made out of glass, I swear it would shatter.

Hawk must read my pain because he curses and pulls me over to the sofa to sit with him. "Kotah, I love you. You," he repeats, placing his warm hand on my chest. "This you. The man who's sweet and giving and everything I never thought I deserved or could have in my life."

"I love you too, but that's the point."

He nods. "Yeah, that's the point. I don't want or need you to be anything you aren't. I never want you to *try* to enjoy sex with me. That would ruin it for both of us."

"But you have appetites for more. I've seen how happy you are after you and Jaxx spend private time together. I want that too."

"Then here we are. Let's spend private time together. And if you like seeing how happy I am after a great session with one of my mates, you should have seen me this morning. I had a smile on my face all morning in my office thinking about pleasuring you in the night."

"But we didn't even have sex."

He smiles and his brow arches in that appraising way of his. He's probably wondering what's wrong with me. He takes my hand and the flash of emotion I feel through my gift is a shock. He's opening his emotions more than he ever has.

He's taking down his walls… for me.

"Nakotah Northwood, I love you the way we are. I'll say it as often as you need to hear it, but I *will* prove it to you."

"I know you love me, but… I want to be enough for you. You are a male of certain tastes and expectations." The confusion in his gaze makes me want to sew my lips together. "Sorry, I'm ruining this."

His gaze softens and he shakes his head. "You're not ruining anything. You're pure of heart and honest. The truth is, I'm the problem here, not you. You're perfect."

Touching as we are, I feel a rush of vulnerability creep into him. I meet his gaze, and yes, the panic he's feeling is there in his eyes. "Kotah, I'm going to confess something to you that I haven't told Calli or Brant and

I'd prefer it remains private."

"Alright."

"When I'm with Jaxx, it's not what the three of you think. It's not me being the dom… I give him all the power. I submit to him entirely and he's the dominant. The joy and happiness you see in me after being with him is because he gives me something I need. He's rough and punishing—at my request—and it works for me."

My mouth falls open. "I never would've guessed."

"My point is that I told Jaxx what I need, and he trusts me and loves me enough to listen. It's perfect when we're like that because it lets his more dominant traits ascend and I give up control for a few hours. It works with us."

"But not with me?"

"Kink and BDSM are a way of life I chose a long time ago to avoid the emotional connection I wasn't ready to accept. I don't want that with you. This is what I want with you." He looks at our joined hands and for the first time, there are no emotional barriers.

"Trust me and love me enough to listen. Really hear me. When we're together, it's perfect. You *are* everything I want." He closes the gap between us, wrapping an arm around me and pulling me to straddle him on the sofa.

"Kotah, you heal my soul and fill me with hope and contentment. I don't want that to change. Naturally, we get different things from different lovers, but that doesn't negate what the others offer. Do you want me to twist myself up and try to sex you the way Brant would or

Jaxx would?"

I swallow, realizing how stupid that sounds. Some genius scholar I am. "No. I'm sorry."

"Don't be sorry. I'm honored you love me enough to want to please me as much as you do. Just do that by being true to who you are. Despite us having a *lot* of sex, you were a virgin three months ago. This is new to you. Don't ever be anyone but yourself in the bedroom and we'll both be happy."

Cue another round of tears burning behind my eyes. "Shit. I'm sorry," I say wiping my eyes and blinking them away. "I'm not usually so emotional."

"And no more apologizing. You've had a rough week, and this is where we are. If tears fall that's fine. If we hurt and disagree and need to iron tough topics out, that's fine. Because in the end, we'll always pull ourselves together and be better than ever. And hopefully… have make-up sex."

I let that sink in as he cups my jaw and rubs a gentle thumb over my lips. "That is… if you'd like that."

My wolf surges forward and a growl rips from my chest. "Yes, please. I would like that very much."

Hawk kisses like he lives life—with no apology for who he is. His teeth nip, his tongue invades, and his erection presses hard against my abdomen as he pulls me closer. With my face gripped from both sides, his fingers dig into my jaw.

His barriers are still down, and I want him to feel how much it means to me—how much I need him to want to be like this with me.

I transfer my emotions into him, sending him my

desire, my joy, and my relief.

His kiss faulters and when he pulls back and looks me in the eyes, there is nothing there but raw emotion. "You are my soul, Wolf. I love you to the depth and breadth of my soul."

Hawk

Fuck me. The kid is too much. He's an open book of goodness and trust. He doesn't begin to understand the fucked-up-ness of me as a mate. Still, I'm *waaay* too invested to turn back now. He doesn't need to change to be what I need him to be. He's got that backward. The onus of changing is all mine.

"Grab the lube from the drawer and get us set up."

While he does as I ask, I lay Calli's nap blanket over the corner seat of the sectional, shuck off my bottoms, and sit. I accept the small bottle of lube, set it on the backrest, and smile up at Kotah. "Take off those pants and join me, Wolf."

His response is immediate, and I have to keep myself locked down not to chuckle. The kid is an eyeful of beauty, whip-thin, a nice sized cock bobbing in the air between us, and that fucking hair of his—yeah, it does it for me in a big way. "Take the tie out of your hair and let it hang loose."

When he reaches back, I watch the twist and pull of his abs flexing. I grip my cock and savor the sight. He's *waaay* too good for me, but I'm enough of a bastard that it didn't stop me from claiming him.

"Come to me. Straddle my hips and let me kiss you some more." He follows my instruction like a freaking champion.

I lean back in the corner of the couch and he climbs into my lap. His thighs straddle mine and within seconds, we're chest-to-chest and kissing again.

His smooth chest moves over my nipple rings and the gentle tug and rub on the platinum hoops sends a zing of sensation to my sac.

Kotah's got a lot more fire in him than I first anticipated.

Even a vanilla life with him will never be ordinary.

I ease back from our kiss and open the spout of the lube and stroke myself slick. When I'm ready, he raises on his knees and I reach beneath his sac to prep him. The key to great male/male sex is lots of slick and slide.

His eyes roll back as I massage the moisture in… first with one, probing finger, and then two. With eight thousand nerves in the anus, it's no wonder it feels amazing to be stimulated. I owe Jaxx so much for opening my eyes to what that means for the five of us.

Kotah drops his head back and shifts his hands to grip the backrest of the couch on either side of my head. His Adam's apple bobs with deep swallows as I work him in. "Good?"

"Yes. So, good."

I smile at the catch in his voice and the knowledge that I key him up as much as I do. "Look at me wolf."

He's so fucking obedient.

This is what I love with Kotah—the connection.

Gazes locked. Both of us actively involved. Touching. Kissing. Everything is about the two of us being present with each other.

Withdrawing my fingers is a shame, but I make it up to both of us by propping my cock against the stretched opening.

"At your pace, Kotah. Don't rush. I'm so fucking good with slow torture." I grip my cock at the root and let him work his way down my shaft inch by glorious inch. His hips shift and rock as he works himself down.

The hot grip of sliding inside him steals my breath.

Cum leaks out of his crown and I grip his erection, palming him as he rides my cock for his pleasure. The mate in me is content stroking him wet while we play but the alpha in me needs more.

I want to slick things up with our juices.

"I want to fuck you."

"Yes, please."

With my arms around him, I twist to the side and lay him on his back. Still joined, I bring my knees onto the cushions of the couch and push forward. His head falls back as he opens his knees wider to give me space to rock my cock.

The throaty growl his wolf lets off when I start a slow and sensual grind notches up my heart rate.

Oh, fuck yeah. This is what we need.

Chest-to-chest with his cock trapped between our rubbing abdomens, I pick up the pace and start slamming home. With each forward thrust, my balls smack his ass, and the sound of flesh hitting flesh sounds off.

I gather his hair between my fingers and marvel at how beautiful he is. His hair is like chestnut velvet and fans out on the cushions around his head like a fucking halo.

I drop my mouth to his neck and suck on his pulse throbbing against his throat. With all my emotional walls down, I'm lost to the sensation of Kotah. He's doing something with his gift, enhancing the connection we share.

There is no beginning or end to the pleasure. Sexual ecstasy fills me, and surrounds me, and cradles me in its hold.

"I love you, Bastian."

The breath in my lungs exits in a rush and my timing falters. I slow to keep from losing it. I was doing great until he said that. I don't know if it's the total surrender of my emotional guard or a lucky guess that tells him to say that, but it's fucking perfect.

"Tell me again…" I growl against his throat. The solid length of his erection is trapped between our grinding abs and getting a firm rubbing as I work back up to a punishing rhythm. "Just like that, Wolf. Again."

"I love you, Bastian."

I let off a throaty bark and push in hard and fast. My abs burn and the pounding gets wild. To his credit, Kotah braces himself like a warrior. "Too much?"

"No," he gasps, digging his fingers into the fleshy rounds of my ass. "Perfect. Exactly this. I love you wild for me."

The world dissolves and there is only me and my mate. A tingling heat rushes through me and it twangs our mating bond. The tie that binds us thickens and even though I claimed him before, this is something on another level—something I didn't even know I was capable of.

I gasp as my release erupts and my hips convulse. Thrusting forward hard, I lock in place and arc back, grunting as I come hard. Fuck yes, this is what we needed.

When we're like this, all is right in the world.

Fuck that… there is no world.

There's just my wolf and me.

CHAPTER EIGHT

Kotah

It's after eight when I wake, snuggled on the sofa with Hawk. My cheek is resting on his chest and the steady beating of his heart softly whispers in my ear. I don't stir. I lay there, breathing his scent deep into my soul, staring at the little platinum ring pierced through his nipple. I will live and die thanking the Powers for giving me the mates I have.

At first, I think he's asleep, but then the feather-light touch of his fingers caresses my bare back. It trails a seductive line from my shoulder blades, down my spine, and over the rise of my hip. When he gets to the downward slope of my ass, his touch changes direction and comes back up.

He's playing with my hair.

My tough guy, corporate raider, alpha is playing with my hair. Too sexy. "Did you sleep?" I ask, not willing to move and lose this connection.

"I did. Very well."

I press my lips against the inked span of his chest

and look up to catch him watching me. "Thank you for last night."

The smile he blesses me with is easily the most contented look I've ever seen on his face. "I was serious when I said you feed my soul, Kotah. You soothe me like no other and I cherish that. You only ever have to be you."

As simple as those words sound, it's nice to hear. In a lifetime of people looking at me and expecting me to be what they want or need me to be, to have mates who love me for the man I truly am is a gift.

Hawk's stomach growls and I press a hand on the ridged planes of his abs. "I suppose we cannot live on love alone. How about omelets for breakfast? I'll cook and you can make those calls to arrange our trip to Pennsylvania."

"Sounds good. You should check in with your sister too. I know how upset she is about your mother, but if she and Doc want to come with us, it could take her mind off things. Maybe working toward thwarting my father might give her some peace until we have more info on your mom."

I roll to the edge of the sofa, find my lounge pants, and pull them on. "Since the Fae Council and the Prime duties are shut down right now anyway, I don't think she's tied to anything here. I'll ask her."

"Oh, and please ask them not to mention where we're going. We've got a leak somewhere and I'm tired of my father being one step ahead of us."

"My sister's loyalty isn't in question, is it?"

"No, no. Not at all. I merely want to play it close to

the vest. My father has been half a step ahead of us all along and it's pissing me off. It's coming to a head though—I feel it."

Calli

"Hey, kitten, are you feelin' okay, babe?"

I blink awake and am lost in the concern in Jaxx's warm turquoise gaze. It's like looking into the tropical waters of the most exotic holiday destination and wanting to dive right in. "Hey, puss. Why the long face?"

"No reason. If you tell me you're good, all will be well."

I straighten the covers and wipe the saliva off my cheek. "Why wouldn't I be okay? What's up?"

"It's after ten. You've been sleepin' for twelve hours. Hawk and I want you to get up and get some food and drink into you. We're worried that maybe you didn't carb load enough after the battle yesterday. We don't want you slippin' into another coma."

I shake my head and sit up. "No, I'm good. I feel fine. I feel better than fine. Maybe I needed a recharge. We've been run ragged lately. I didn't miss anything important, did I?"

By the guilty look on his face, the answer to that is obviously yes. "Hawk and Kotah came to a few hot and heavy realizations around three. It woke Brant and me up. We got started, thinkin' you'd wake up and join in, but you missed the whole thing."

"Huh… weird. Usually, I'm the first one to key up when the mating bond is triggered."

"Thus, my concern," he says, pressing his lips to my forehead and holding them there as if he's assessing my temperature. "You're sure you're okay?"

"Yep. I'm great." I scootch off the bed and grab some clothes. "Do we have a plan for today?"

"The plane is fueled and ready on the tarmac. Hawk and Kotah came up with an inspired theory in the wee hours."

"So, it wasn't all about mating fun?"

"Nope. There was a definite meetin' of the minds before the meetin' of the males."

"And what's their theory?"

Jaxx gives me a brief update on a property in Pennsylvania and then heads downstairs to let the guys know I'm up and getting ready. I tell him to pack me a to-go breakfast and do the speed round shower and dress routine. I forego makeup and give my hair a quick blow dry before pulling it into a ponytail.

Look at me. A phoenix girl on the go.

Fifteen minutes later, I'm jogging down the stairs. Lukas is chatting with Hawk over at the coffee machine and Doc and Keyla are sitting at the table with Kotah.

"Ready to roll. Sorry, guys. I didn't mean to be the lazy daisy on the team."

"No apology, beautiful," Brant says, intercepting me by the table to kiss me. "If your body didn't need the sleep, you would've woken up on your own."

Everyone has their shoes on, and I feel even worse about them sitting around all morning waiting on me. "Next time wake me up earlier. I don't need to sleep all morning if we've got things to do."

Kotah sends me an apologetic look. "We did wake you up, *Chigua*. Or, at least, we tried. You growled at Hawk and told him to go away, and an hour later told Brant to shove his promises of bacon up his ass."

My mouth falls open. "I did not."

Brant chuckles and flashes me a toothy grin. "Oh, you did. I only wish I had my phone ready, so I could've caught the look of disgust that went with it for posterity. I'll be ready next time though."

Heat flares in my cheeks and I can't face the amused looks of our friends. I drop my gaze to the floor and focus on getting my shoes on and getting ready to leave. "Sorry. I don't remember that."

Jaxx chuckles. "It's okay, kitten. If you were exhausted, we'd rather give you the time you need to rest up than have you crash. We never want to go through that again."

I meet Hawk's gaze and offer him a reassuring smile. "It won't happen. I promise."

He nods. "We'll make sure of it. Now, before we leave. Take five minutes in the library and see if you can connect with Riley. Let her know we're heading to these coordinates and will try, once again, to find a way to make contact with StoneHaven and her realm."

I take the paper with the coordinates and head to the library. "I'll try, but don't hold your breath. I think that whatever Riley was trying to hide from and avoid, has forced her into hiding. There's no way she'd drop off the map like this if she could help it."

"See what happens, Spitfire. Destiny has a few surprises left in store for us, I'm sure. Might as well have the most people on our side as possible."

Jaxx

The flight to the property in Pennsylvania takes almost three hours. We're comfy in Hawk's plane and quite at home. The eight of us have become quite a happy entourage and after yesterday's ceremony, we're all ready to get away from the palace for a bit.

Our inflight entertainment is Brant playing the part of our steward and offering mile-high opportunities, while Hawk tries to brief us all on who's who in the Black Knight camp.

"You look a lot like your father," Calli says as we study the picture of Sabastian Senior on the monitor. "It's that creased brow of harsh disdain and those icy gray eyes."

"I grew up wishing I looked like my mother," Hawk says, shifting his weight in his seat to pull out his wallet.

Lukas smiles. "Oh, now there was a beautiful woman. Liza was tall and elegant and had the warmest hugs of any of the magicals my parents visited when I was a kid."

"She did. And man, she loved kids. If she hadn't gotten sick, I bet I would've had four or five younger siblings."

Hawk's smiles are coming easier every day. He pulls out a small picture of a radiant woman squatting down with her toddler to point at ducks on a pond.

I look at it, take a picture of it with my phone, and then pass it to Calli. "How old are you here," she asks.

"The date's on the back. Four, I think?"

"You're right. She's stunning."

"Losing her was a true loss," Lukas says.

At the mention of Elizaveta's disease, they both sober. I forget sometimes that Lukas is a Squire of the London Order of the Guild of Mages and his family served Hawk's mother.

Hawk looks like waxing philosophical is hitting a bit too close to home, and then he flips to the next photo. "I guess I did get one sibling. You remember my half-brother, Hunter. Spineless, entitled, inflated opinion of himself."

I frown at the face of a man who looks nothing like Hawk. He doesn't have the internal strength of our mate and certainly doesn't have that core code of honor that Hawk lives by. "I think you got off easy with him. He was in your private circle for years and could've done a dozen things to you and gotten away with it."

Lukas and Hawk both nod.

"And these are the missing Fae Council members. We're currently placing them in the enemy camp, but the jury is still out on that."

Hawk flips through a few more slides and then turns off the monitor.

"Do we know who owns the land on the opposite side of the river yet?" Kotah asks. "Do they know we're coming?"

Hawk shakes his head. "I came across a convoluted chain of shell companies. I didn't have time to track through the paperwork, so it's a case of ask forgiveness not permission on this one. Besides, the area we're targeting is so remote, there likely isn't anyone around. We should have no troubles."

Brant snorts. "He says, not believing his own bullshit."

Hawk shrugs. "Where there's life there's hope."

"Where there's smoke there's fire."

Calli laughs. "Where there's fire there's me."

"Where there's you, there's us, *Chigua,*" Kotah adds.

I finish the round-robin. "And where there's us, there's usually trouble."

"Preach," Brant says, popping up his fist for a bump. "But maybe this time it'll be different."

We all look at Brant and bust up laughing.

"Or maybe not."

We land without incident and two trucks are waiting at the airport as usual. The five of us pile into our truck and buckle up. Hawk and Brant in the front, Calli and Kotah in the middle, and I'm stretched out in the back.

Lukas, Doc, and Keyla take the other truck with the two FCO drivers who brought the trucks and will now join the expedition as back up security.

"What's our plan to get into the site?" I ask as the truck slows and takes a sideroad. "By the aerial shots, it looked wild and really, darn remote."

Hawk grins. "Oh, it is. We're going in on the river."

"Boats?" Brant asks, looking alarmed.

"A raft, actually, but a big, sturdy, raft. The river bottom is too rocky and uneven for boats."

Brant's growl fills the truck. "Hello, living anchor

here."

"I haven't forgotten, Bear. Don't worry. I've got you and Doc covered. We're not going to lose you, boys."

Brant lifts his chin and puts on a front but he's not fooling anyone. Our bear isn't afraid of anything—except water.

"We've got you, my man. I'm the water shard, remember? I won't let you drown. And hey, if the river bottom is too rocky for boat motors, it's shallow enough that you should be able to stand up."

"Unless it's one of the uneven points and I sink… or I get swept away by the current."

"You won't get swept away, Bear," Hawk says. "The guide I spoke to says this river is smooth as glass. Nothing to worry about."

"And speaking of the mating crystals," Calli says, turning sideways in her seat to look at all of us. "When is it going to do its thing and become a pendant of unlocked power?"

We all look to Kotah. He's our man with the answers and has researched the phoenix lore more than any of us. "The ancient fae tongue is a hermetic and sylvan language which is intuitive and flexibly woven. When translated the description given evolves into something like, "When the quint is bound and five become one, the binding of power shall be undone."

Calli shrugs. "Well? Didn't we do that? We've all mated with everyone. We're all on the same page for life, love, and purpose. We are one, aren't we?"

I take her hand from where it rests on the back of

her seat and bring her knuckles to my lips. "The mating crystals don't think so, kitten. Not yet anyway."

"Could they be broken?" Brant asks. "They were magically sitting around in the ether for gods only know how long. Maybe they need a jump start or something."

"What jumpstarts magical soul crystals?" Calli asks.

Kotah pulls his out of where it hangs against his chest beneath his shirt and examines it. "Putting them all together?"

I dip my hand into the collar of my shirt and pull mine out as well. "Can't hurt to try."

Hawk and Brant each fish out their pendants and hand them to Calli. She holds them together and closes her eyes. "Come on, mighty fae crystals. Do your thing."

We all watch and wait but nothing happens.

"Well, crud," she says, deflated. "Maybe all five of us have to be touching or something when we focus on the crystals. Five become one, right?"

Calli holds the crystals and I take her hand. Brant touches Hawk's arm while he drives and reaches back to hold Kotah's hand, who, in turn, touches Calli and me.

Nothing happens.

Calli frowns, sorts out the pendants, and hands them back. "Why can't anything be easy for once?"

I throw up my hands. "Destiny, am I right?"

We're all still chuckling about that when Hawk pulls off the graveled road and stops beside the other truck. We're in a worn patch of land, parked in front of an outfitter group set up on the bank of a wide river.

I'm kinda jazzed about rafting but keep that in check

for the sake of those of us who are much less enthused.

Hawk looks over at me when I jump out. He tilts his head over to where Brant is breaking the bad news to Doc and the avian is all smiles. "At least life is never boring."

I laugh. "With us, I doubt boring will ever be a word in our vocabulary."

Brant

What. The. Fuck. As we all pile out of the truck, I'm considering opting out and waiting here. River rafting? "Okay, seriously guys, this is probably my worst nightmare come to life. I don't know that I can do this. Maybe I can hike in, or get a dirt bike and ride in."

Hawk looks hella apologetic when he shakes his head. "It would take you five or six hours to hike it and dirt bikes would not only give away our element of surprise but also disturb the fae species which make this land their home."

"What kind of fae are we talking about because I'm pretty charming. I could explain—"

"The colony closest to the river is the fire dervishes."

I wince. "Oh, those little fuckers are nasty."

"Yeah, no shit."

Calli wraps an arm around my hip and laces her thumb through my belt loop. "We'll strap you into a life jacket and as an absolute worst-case scenario, I can go full phoenix and pluck you out of the water. It'll be like when we escaped Hawk's office tower, except without all the bullet holes."

"And that worked out well enough," Jaxx says. "Sex on the deck, magical healin', badda-bing you're all fixed up."

I shake my head. "If this is your idea of a pep talk, you guys suck at it. Seriously."

Lukas returns from speaking to the raft outfitters and shrugs. "What's the word? Are we doing this?"

All eyes fall on me and I look at Doc. He's not much happier than I am, but he also isn't as big or heavy. There's a chance he could navigate the water. There's no chance for me.

I curse. "Fuckety-fuck. I don't want to do this."

"Then don't," Kotah says, gripping my wrist with his magic touch and sending me a wave of calm. "If we're going downriver, they'll have to drive down to pick us up, so stay with the crew and we'll meet up in a few hours. It's okay if you skip this one, isn't it guys?"

They all front and give me the okay.

"Of course," Calli says. "Stay with the crew and we'll meet up downriver. Kotah's right, as usual. That works too."

Oh, how I want to take the out.

But deep inside me, my bear is vibrating with fury at the thought of choosing fear over my mates. "Fuck me. No. I'll go. But if I drown, I'm never forgiving you guys. Seriously. You'll all be on my shit list for eternity and I *will* haunt you."

CHAPTER NINE

Calli

We get Brant and Doc decked out with their PFD life vests and each of them opts for a ring buoy around their waist as well. Once Brant is settled in the middle of the raft, the rest of us vest up, push off, and climb in.

The river isn't too fast-flowing, but our guide says it gets a little quicker closer to where we're going. Thankfully, Brant isn't listening.

The guide steers from the back of the boat. He has two long paddles anchored in place and he keeps us in the center of the river as we practice our paddling and matching strokes.

Lukas, Hawk, Jaxx, and one of the FCO guys have all done this before, so that makes me feel a little more confident that between all of us, we've got this.

Well, that and the fact that there's a professional guide on board to navigate.

"Brant, do you think you and Doc can check the coordinates now and then if the rest of us are paddling? And maybe keep your eyes on the landscape in case we run into any trouble."

Brant and Doc each have a firm hold on two tether straps attached to the floor of the boat. Brant twists his wrist to check if he can see the screen on his FCO watch and then swallows. "Yeah, I think so."

Hawk squeezes his shoulder and pats his arm. "Good stuff, Bear. You're doing great. You too, Doc."

I try not to snort. Where Brant's panic is loud and dramatic, Doc has withdrawn into a silent scowl and is no doubt unable to speak because his jaw is clamped so tightly shut.

"You're both rocking this," Keyla says. "It'll be over before you know it and you'll have the story to tell Ben and Margo the next time you go home to the ranch."

The bears don't acknowledge her attempt to cheer them up. "It's quite peaceful out here, isn't it?"

Yeah-no. Still nothing.

"Look how calm the water is. Nothing to worry about."

They don't respond, but the fact that we're floating along on pristine and still water has to make it easier.

Kotah smiles up at the mid-afternoon sun and then at his sister. "It is peaceful. I prefer having soil beneath my claws but yes, for an adventure with friends and my mates, it's a nice experience."

"I can think of fifty nicer experiences for the five of us to share," Brant growls.

Jaxx chuckles, matching my stroke into the water with a wink. "Let me guess, the first one is sex."

"Actually, yes."

I chuckle at the guide at the back of the boat. He's got his eyes firmly locked on the waterway ahead of us, but he's about to get an earful, I'm sure.

"Then what, Brant," Kotah says. "What would your next pick on the list be?"

"Sharing a roast beef dinner."

The four of us start laughing and I can't even look at anyone else in the boat.

"Why is that funny?" Keyla asks. "Or is that TMI?"

"Wicked TMI, girlfriend," I say.

"Okay Brant," Hawk says, chuckling, "what's your next experience better than this and it can't be sex. Our friends already have to endure enough around us without torturing them and our poor guide with awkward images."

"All right, Jaxx's drinking games."

Jaxx snorts. "Fun… but also always lead to sex."

"Physical combat training," I add.

The five of us laugh.

Keyla groans. "Seriously, you guys? Does everything you do lead to sex?"

Lukas grunts. "Afraid so. I need to find a quint of my own and make them pay. They deserve a little taste of what it's like to be on the outside of a fivesome."

"Hells, yes," I say, loving that idea. "Lukas, seriously, if I had any friends I liked enough to set you up with, I totally would, but my only bestie is Riley and we're not even sure she's real, so there's that."

Hawk chuckles. "I've accused Lukas of having imaginary girlfriends before. Riley's not a total write-off."

That gets a laugh from us and earns Hawk a middle-finger salute from Lukas. The important thing is Brant is now chuckling and his knuckles are no longer clenched so tightly that the blood is being pinched out.

"I've got one," I say, dipping my oar and pulling it through the water. "Paintball training. We played capture the flag all afternoon. It was fun and *didn't* lead to sex."

"Despite the flags we captured."

I roll my eyes as the guys chuckle. Yeah, the goal was to find my undies hidden in the forest. Oh well, let them yuck it up. At least Brant's not losing his shit.

"Dinner with Ben and Margo," Kotah adds. "It was fun to share a meal with your foster parents and see you in your family home with your sleuth."

I turn from where I'm paddling. "Man, does your family eat. I've never seen so much food."

"Dancing at the Rusty Spur was a good time," Jaxx says.

"Hells yeah, that was—"

Lukas lets off a curse behind us and I spin—Gun!

Bang

The crack of the gun discharging echoes in my head as Jaxx launches and knocks me to the side. The boat rocks as two high-strung bears dive onto the bottom of the boat. Lukas unsheaths his thigh knife and impales our guide and Hawk shoves him over the hull.

My mind is swimming as I try to catch up.

Then I register Jaxx's frantic movement six inches from where I was sitting. "Shit, we're hit!"

Jaxx

"Shit, we're hit!" I toss my paddle into the boat and press my hands over the tear in the thick nylon hull. That fucker tried to take out Calli. If I wasn't holding my hands over a hole in the hull, I'd dive overboard so I could kill the bastard myself.

A rifle shot echoes from our right and my heart thunders even harder. "Kitten, get down."

"We're sitting ducks," Brant snaps, his voice more growl than words.

"Barron," Lukas snaps. "Plug that hole. Kotah, take his spot to keep us balanced. Bears stay where you are. Jaxx, once he's got his hands over the tear, I need you back here to steer us downriver."

"Fuck downriver," Brant says. "We need to get to the bank and get out of this dingy deathtrap."

Lukas isn't listening. He's turned to the back of the boat speaking in magical tongues.

I catch sight of Brant's eyes and a whole world of panic hits. "Kotah, you need to calm the bears down right now. If they lose their hold on their wild sides, I guarantee this will become Shit's Creek in a hot minute."

Keyla meets Doc's gaze and offers him a comforting smile. "Please, hold on. We don't want two irate bears in the middle of this raft."

Kotah drops his paddle on the floor and kneel-crawls closer to Brant and Doc. Grabbing each of them with his outstretched hands, our Omega closes his eyes and the bears' eyes roll closed too.

Thank you, baby Yoda.

With that pending disaster averted, we all get back to the other problems—a hole in the boat and a sniper shooting at us. I have no idea what Lukas is doing, but the tingle of his magic raises the hair on my arms.

There's no time to dwell.

Hawk crawls into my position and his hands press over mine. I give him possession of the hole and shift to take Lukas's position at the back, grabbing onto the stern mount handles to steer. Another shot rings off and we all duck.

Crack. The incoming bullet hits a protective field and falls to the rising flow of water.

"Well done, Lukas," Calli says.

Hawk is hanging over the side of the boat, calling on his magical side. He doesn't have the juice Lukas does, but his mother did give him access to a few tricks.

Hopefully, Raft Patching 101 is one of them.

As soon as I've got a hold on the stern handles, Lukas drops to his knees on the floor of the raft and stretches over the side to the river behind us.

In answer to his call, the waters rise in a rush and the serene river behind us is now white with rapids. *Shit.* I watch the rush of whitewater coming and grip the handles tighter. My heart pounds against my ribcage as I wait for the thundering current to hit.

Right before we're caught in the tidal wave, I dig in. "Hold on, everyone."

The tsunami knocks us hard and we pitch forward in a rough wave. Everyone lurches but has a good hold and soon the momentum drags us into its wake.

I fight the force of the rush, trying to keep the raft in the center of the river.

Another shot cracks.

It bounces off the protective field. “I seriously love you right now, Lukas. Mad, manly love.”

Hawk rolls back to his knees and grabs my abandoned paddle. “The good news is the tear is fixed.”

“What’s the bad news,” Brant growls. “Beyond us getting shot and drowning in this fucking river.”

Hawk lurches to the side as the raft shimmies and bounces. “No one’s drowning, Bear, I promised you. The bad news is they know we’re here. Odds are they’re set up to take us out where we planned to land the raft and go inland. We’ll have to dock upriver and hump it to where we think the portal gate location sits now.”

“News flash. Getting off this fucking river early is *not* bad news.”

Calli is paddling hard as water sprays up in her face. “At least they’ll be on the wrong side of the river, won’t they?”

“I’m hoping so.” Hawk pushes a floating branch away with his paddle. “But Hunter was at FCO long enough to know I requested a science team to investigate the diverting of this river. He might’ve come to the same conclusion as I did.”

I grunt. “Unlikely, hotness. Your half-brother is a lazy tool. I doubt he has a quarter of the instincts you have.”

Hawk flashes me a sexy grin. “You flirting with me, puss? I have to warn you, I do love adrenaline moments.”

Brant’s bear lets off a furious growl. ”Seriously? Can we focus on the clusterfuck that is our lives?”

Despite Brant’s panic, we’ve got control of the raft

and are shooting fast and furious toward our destination.

"Check the coordinates, Bear. Dock us one or two miles upriver from our original goal. Tell us when we need to shift left and look for a place to land this thing."

Brant scowls. "You expect me to do the math when I'm having a coronary?"

Hawk chuckles. "Or switch places with me and paddle."

Brant lets off another growl. "Asshole."

Hawk

Call me sadistic, but Brant in a panicked rage is kind of funny. I know phobias and fear are nothing to laugh at, but there's no way I'd let him drown. We have a greater chance of being shot or blown out of the water by launched missiles—which is not out of the question. My father's militia seems to favor that as a weapon of mass destruction.

"How are you doing on those coordinates, Bear," I ask, fighting the magically boosted waves as we are propelled down the river. "Are we close?"

"We're three miles out in total, so if you want to land one to two miles upstream and a raft like this one moves at around nine miles an hour we'll be in position in about ten minutes, give or take."

"So, not time to steer left yet," Jaxx says.

"Not yet, Jaguar," Brant says. "We should watch the shoreline. If we see a break in the bank we can use as a landing point, we'd be wise to take it when we see it."

I smile. The bear might be full of bluster and fight when he's scared but give him a problem to solve and people to take care of, and he's focused once again.

Calli said it a few weeks ago when Brant was working on his mating bonds. He's our strength, but that goes deeper than his muscles. His truest strength is his determination and commitment to protecting the people around him.

Even if he's scared shitless.

"Well done, Bear. Keep your eyes on the horizon and let us know when we're getting close."

"How did Black Knight know we were coming?" Calli asks. She's at the front of the boat across from me, paddling like a trooper. "We didn't tell anyone, and we still have people shooting at us."

"Lukas will need to work on tracking that once we get back. The leak must be in my logistics team or my vehicle pool. Or maybe the enemy was already here to do their gate destructo act. Or maybe it wasn't them and just some crazy fae that doesn't like rafters. I honestly don't know."

My gut tells me everything that happens to us and around us is my father's doing but that might be paranoia more than reality. Life taught me hard lessons on not underestimating how cruel and driven the man can be. I might've gone the other way and be giving him too much credit.

"Okay, Jaxx," Brant says, pulling me out of my musings. "Start easing left and I'll watch for a landing spot downstream."

Jaxx works the stern paddles, gradually moving us to the left of the ever-bending river.

"I researched the shoreline of the river on Google

Earth this morning," Kotah says, paddling behind me. "As of the time the last aerial shots were taken, there seemed to be a large tree that fell along the bank close to where we might need to be. If we can't find an open spot, maybe we could grab hold of it somehow and use it to pull ourselves up."

"I'd prefer to have access to the forest and take the raft right out of the water," I say. "Hiding our insertion point is an advantage if people are looking for us."

Jaxx nods. "Yeah, if they know we're coming and then we don't show up, they'll backtrack. This raft is like a giant yellow flag for them to find us."

Calli stops paddling and flops against the hull for a rest. "The more we can do to slow them down the better. I'm still not one hundy on what I'm supposed to do to open a gate."

"If there's even is a gate to open," Jaxx says.

"I think there is," I say, unsure where the sudden optimism is coming from. "I know that's a big if, but I believe in us, down to the marrow of my bones."

"Aren't bird bones hollow?" Brant asks.

I roll my eyes at the bear. "Now who's the asshole?"

Brant chuckles and points. "There's Kotah's tree. Are we taking that as our inland route or passing it for the hope of finding a clearer landing point?"

No one offers up any opinions, so I bite the bullet. "Take it, Jaxx. Get us over there. Lukas, maybe you can whip up a concealment spell on this giant rubber ducky so we can keep our position hidden long enough to get things done."

Lukas pegs me with a stink-eyed glare. "Yes, sir. I'll

get right on that as soon as I take down the protective field keeping us from getting shot and release the power of the river that I've been calling and commanding for the past fifteen minutes."

I chuckle and hold up my hands. "It was just a request."

CHAPTER TEN

Calli

While Hawk, Lukas, and Kotah work on securing the raft and glamouring it out of sight, Keyla and Doc get some distance, and Jaxx and I tend to Brant. Once our bear's feet are on solid ground, I figure we'll be good. *Wrong.* His massive frame bursts to bear and he lifts his maw to the air to let off a piss your pants roar.

"Alrighty then. Not fine."

He grunts and stomps into the trees, snapping twigs and scaring the locals.

Jaxx catches the worry on my expression and smiles. "He'll be fine in a bit. Give him a chance to burn off some of his anxiety and calm down."

"We should stick close to him. If people are out here with rifles, I don't want anyone shooting him thinking he's a raging bear."

Jaxx chuckles. "The people out here shooting are likely more interested in shooting us than a bear. We've got a few minutes while they work on the dingy. He'll be back by then."

I don't share Jaxx's optimism.

"Okay, you do you. I want to go see if maybe I can help calm him down."

Jaxx breaks into a smile. "You can try."

The two of us tromp off in the direction Brant's bear took and soon come to broken ground with a rock formation jutting up from the forest floor.

The huff and growl of my bear are unmistakable. Rounding the upcropping rocks, my breath catches. Brant's in fine form, his bear seeming bigger than usual in his current state of fury and fluster. Standing eye level in front of me, his massive, boxy face and golden eyes strike me to my very core.

"Hey, bear. You okay?" Jaxx asks.

He twitches his black nose and lets off another long-suffering groan. It vibrates inside my chest. When I pat the spot where I feel his anguish, he lumbers forward and presses his forehead against my chest.

My fingers sink into his muzzle and scrub his cheek. His pelt is thick, the fur long and luxurious. "I'm sorry the river part was rough on you, big guy."

"It'll take him a minute to shift back," Jaxx says, his voice laced with understanding. "When we're hurt or worked up and retreat into our base selves our animal instincts surge forward. He'll be raw and aggressive until he burns it off."

I press my cheek against his head. "That's fine. He has every right to be upset. We'll deal."

I nuzzle into Brant's neck and breathe him in. "You smell good, Bear. Like evergreen trees and summer sun."

Pressed against his sturdy frame my skin tingles

when he shifts back to my mate. My very naked, very aroused mate.

He moves in with predatory strength and primal sexuality and lifts me off the ground. The tearing of fabric spells the end of my blouse and Jaxx manages to get my pants down my thighs fast enough to save them.

Even though he's standing before me as a man, Brant's eyes are glowing the solid gold of his bear.

He'll be raw and aggressive until he burns it off.

"Tell me if you need me to alpha stop this, kitten."

"No!" Brant snarls.

"No," I say, gripping Brant's shoulders as he grapples ahold of me to block Jaxx. "No, I'm good. He won't hurt me."

Strong fingers knot in my hair and I gasp as his mouth seizes mine. His tongue pries my lips apart at the same time he presses my back against a moss-covered rock wall and splits my legs.

My pulse hammers in my veins and a rush of hot moisture soaks my core.

He breathes in deep and his growl rumbles through his chest to mine. "You cream for me."

"All for you, Bear."

This is Brant, more bear than man. He tips his head back and his lips curl. "They shot at you. Tried to take my mate from me."

"I'm whole. Prove to your bear that I'm strong and healthy." We've been through this enough that I know if their wildling sides get triggered about my safety, nothing will soothe them until I'm marked and mated once again. "Fuck me, Bear."

Before the words are out of my mouth, he sets me on the ground, spins me around, and bends me toward the rockface. Rough hands spread my thighs as his crown pushes inside.

I cry out, shock and arousal warring in my mind. Brant's always so careful. He primes me. He stretches my muscles before he enters me. Not today.

"You okay, kitten?"

"Yes," I say, the invasion stealing my breath. "Gawd, you're so big, Bear." With my palms splayed against the jagged surface of the rock, I brace for what's next.

"Tell me to fuck you again." The masculine demand in his voice triggers a pulsing clench in my womb.

"Fuck me, Bear."

He grips my hips and invades me with a rough thrust. I cry out, but the pain of being stretched too much too quickly is soon replaced by the burn of slide and glide.

I'm so wet.

This man—this beast isn't Brant—but it is.

A part of him, anyway.

"You like that, beautiful? Do you need me hard and deep? Do you need what I can give you?"

"Yes."

His body, hard and muscled, hits me from behind. The penetration is pure, scalding pleasure. He shifts his stance and fills me again. And again. And again.

His growl bounces off the rocks and trees around us, the guttural vibration bearing no resemblance to his usual easy-going tone. His foot inside my ankle spreads my legs wider as he thrusts deeper, driving harder.

The clenching muscles of my sex tense around him. The building pressure of my release ratcheted nearer. My nails dig at the moss, grasping for purchase to ride out this maelstrom.

Brant isn't an alpha, but that doesn't mean he's not downright aggressive. He thrusts inside me, over and over, and with each hit, I push against the rock. My hands are scraped and probably bleeding, the muscles in my arms burning. This is wild and carnal and I love everything about it.

"I love you rough bear. Really fuck me rough."

The forest erupts in the slap of flesh and the grunts of pleasure. I can't hold them back. I don't want to. My skin ignites, and I know without opening my eyes that I'm glowing. My woman aflame comes forward now when I let my wild side loose.

And I love it.

I flip my head back and grind my clit against each incoming hit. A sharp, keening zing releases with each penetration and my need tightens viciously.

More. Harder. Wilder.

"Gawd, yes…"

A fiery burst of pleasure shatters inside me.

My orgasm pours through me in a scorching wave. I cry out, lost to the primal connection between me and my bear. I sag forward, riding out the tidal waves of release.

So good.

I pant hard, trying to get reacquainted with oxygen.

My legs give out as Brant withdraws but I don't fall. He has me in his arms and spins me, so my back is against the rock wall and I'm wrapping my legs around his waist.

"I want to kiss you."

I wrap my arms around his neck and groan as he reclaims his place. His cock slides in and wow, I'm going to be sore. Doesn't matter.

My phoenix side will heal me within the hour.

Brant crushes me in his embrace. His arms wrap around me, guiding me up and down the length of his shaft, as his mouth finds the hollow at the base of my throat.

This is the best kind of torture.

He pulls back enough for me to see the anguish in his eyes. "I want to… I need to…"

A shiver chills my bare skin. "Whatever it is, my answer is *yes*. I want all of you. No holds. No manners. I want your wild side, Bear."

I watch as his canines lengthen, and he lowers his mouth toward my shoulder. A sharp scrape over my flesh sends another shiver up my spine. He nips the sensitive skin above my collarbone, his gaze locked with mine. "May I?"

The need is wild in his gaze and I swallow. "Yes."

His face grows savage with lust as he closes his eyes. White daggers puncture my flesh and the pain that sears me is so wildly out of control, I convulse around him in another wave of orgasm.

He moans and starts pumping again.

Rapture explodes along our mating bond and sends

me higher. I was wrong to think of this as wild sex to reassure his bear. This is more than sex.

This is Brant's bear possessing me.

As my orgasm grips and releases, his rhythm shifts from fast to frenetic. Hot breath washes over my shoulder as he pants against my skin. His teeth remain sunken in my flesh.

I'm dizzy as hell. Not from the bite… but yeah, from what it does to me to have him bite me.

With one final growl, his hips pitch forward and lock. He releases his bite, and snarls so loud the echo bounces off the rocks and trees around us.

I tuck my face into the warmth of his neck and revel in the sensation of warm cum coating my throbbing muscles. As a human, I never could've imagined this kind of sensitivity but as a wildling, it's one of my favorite things.

The heady burn to have my mates mark me eases with such primal bliss when they're coming inside me, I crave it day and night. It's the same for them.

There's no way to make sense of it, yet I hope it never ends. By the time his release eases, my legs feel like rubber and my entire body is shaking with worn muscles.

I sense when the bear recedes, and the man regains control. Gentle fingers stroked my shoulder, pausing over the sensitive tissue where he bit me. "I'm sorry I lost control."

I smile up at him and let the glow of my phoenix side recede. "I'm not. Not unless too much pleasure can destroy a person. If that's the case, I might be in trouble."

Jaxx

Once Brant and Calli finish fucking like animals in the forest, I help her get into her pants and offer her my shirt. Technically, it should be Brant who sacrifices his shirt, but that would be a dress on her and not a top. And we still might need to run or fight at any moment, so my shirt is a better choice. Plus, it's not for long. As soon as we get back with the group, Hawk opens one of the travel packs and tosses Calli a shirt.

After almost three months of dealing with Calli's phoenix fire issues, we've learned to pack her backup clothes for whenever we're not close to home.

"All good?" Hawk asks, tossing me my shirt once our girl has covered her girls.

"Brant's bear needed a moment," Calli says, her cheeks flaming red.

"Trust us. We heard."

I chuckle and wrap an arm around Calli, walking her away from the knowing smiles. "Ignore them. We are who we are. No one else gets a vote."

After another ten minutes, the Pennsylvania forest sextacular is forgotten and everyone returns to normal. Kotah and Keyla shift to wolf and are happy to run point and see if there are any dangers in our path.

Brant and Doc break off to chat.

Lukas and Hawk are talking safety and strategy with the two FCO guys Alex and Amir, and that leaves Calli and me to enjoy the forest hike.

"I've never been to Pennsylvania," she says, smiling

at the trees surrounding us. "It's nice."

"It is." The forest is dense, the canopy thick, and the shuffle and scuffle of wildlife rustles all around us. While I prefer the hot sun and the feathered heads of wheat swaying in vast fields, this runs a close second. "It reminds me of the Northwood property."

"Which is probably why Kotah's so happy."

"That and the fact that Keyla's here with him and we're out here doin' our Guardian thing instead of bein' cooped up in the palace assuming his duties as the Fae Prime."

Calli nods. "I don't blame him for that."

"Me either."

We walk a long while in companionable silence before she reaches over and laces her fingers with mine. "I can almost forget there are madmen after us and two realms depending on us to battle the dark forces when we're alone like this."

"Nature has a healing ability all its own." Our joined hands swing between us and when the way narrows or gets clogged up, I use our hold to help her through. Now and then, we catch a glimpse of our wolves or bears in the trees, but for the most part, we're alone in paradise. "How are you feelin' now, kitten? Is your sleepy spell over with?"

Her emerald gaze glitters as she stops our progress. Pushing me up against the closest tree, she leans in and claims my mouth. I'm always good for this kind of an ambush and meet her teasing affection with my own.

Unfortunately, time is not our own.

I end the kiss and ease back, my cat pleased with the

distraction. “So, I take that as a *yes*. You’re feeling good.”

“Great even. I feel strong and happy and in love. I’m hopeful that we’ll succeed. And I’m determined to find Riley. If I had a pack of M&Ms I’d be golden. But other than craving crunchy chocolate, I haven’t a want in the world.”

Good. That’s good.

Still… my cat thinks differently. There’s something off with her and I can’t quite figure out what it is.

“You two done making out?” Hawk calls from ahead.

I waggle my eyebrows and flash Calli a teasing gaze. “Only if we have to be.”

“You do. If we’re waylaid every time one of us sports a stiff cock, we’ll never get to the coordinates.”

I chuckle and get us moving again. “Spoilsport.”

It doesn’t take long before we catch up with Hawk and the others. Hawk’s got an aerial map pulled up on a tablet and is tracking our progress.

“How long will it take for us to get there?” Calli asks.

Hawk hands the tablet to Lukas and offers her a hand to help her up a steep slope. “Wildlings hike at about one mile an hour. According to Brant’s calculations, we’re just over a mile away from where we want to be.”

“Oh, okay.”

The disappointment in her tone is nothing Hawk or I miss. “What is it, Spitfire?”

"Nothing important. I'm good."

He chuckles and shakes his head. "No, you're not. Tell us, please."

"No, I *am* fine. I'm just hungry and we're looking at another three hours or more before we get finished and back to the raft to get out of here."

Hawk stops and turns his back to me. "Jaxx, snacks are in the zipped pocket sealed in the plastic. Pull something out for our girl."

I do as he says and smile at the yellow candy bag. "Ask and ye shall receive my queen. M&M peanuts for you, courtesy of our ever-anticipatory mate."

"Yay! Thank you." She takes the bag, rips the top corner off, and starts popping in the colored chocolates. The smile she beams over at us is like July sunshine and the finest whiskey. "Man, I love you two."

My cat purrs long and loud as her words warm me inside and out. "And we love you."

We continue like that until Kotah and Keyla come barreling past us and shoot off to our left. They're growling and not the happy, tongue-wagging wolves they've been the past hour.

The level of aggression puts us all on notice and we tighten our ranks. "What is it?" Hawk asks, narrowing his gaze on the trees. "Does anyone hear or see anything?"

I shake my head, searching the trees and the surrounding area. "No, but if you boys are good here, I'll check it out."

Hawk, Lukas, and the FCO guys all have their guns drawn, so I squeeze Calli's hand and pull away. Shifting on the fly, the wide pads of my paws come down on the leaves and twigs as I gain speed. After a few more running leaps, I launch into the air, grab hold of an angled tree, and climb for a better vantage point.

Brant and Doc are below, lumbering through the scrub. Other than that, I don't see or hear anything. Certainly, nothing that concerns me.

Still… Kotah's senses are the keenest of all of us, so I don't relax. I trust his wolf and when he blew through here, he wasn't happy. The air tingles in my nose and the hair on the ruff of my neck stands on end.

Magic.

"There's a portal opening," Hawk shouts from below. "Incoming."

He barely gets the warning out as a dozen men spill out of the energy distortion before us. They come through, fully engaged weapons raised and firing.

Calli bursts into flames and gets between the incoming force and Hawk and Lukas. The two of them have their guns out and scramble for cover to return fire. That's if there's anyone left to attack after Calli gets done charbroiling them.

Dropping to the branch below me, I take a run and launch through the air. My cat lets off a roaring *rowl* and I take down two unsuspecting attackers. Protective vests and guns are no defense against speed, strength, and dagger-sharp claws.

I go for the exposed flesh of their throats and they fall without a fight.

A pair of coyotes flank me with a hyena and my cat lets off a rumble of excitement. Finally, a decent challenge.

Wildling to wildling is the stuff of legend.

As the forest erupts in snarls and the crack of gunfire, I dig in and take on my three. The coyotes are quicker than me, but not as strong. The hyena matches me in strength but doesn't have my agility.

The makings of an exciting battle in my mind.

I swipe at one of the hindquarters of a coyote and send him spinning into a tree trunk with a yelp. His battle partners compensate and close in. With two running strides, I leap at a tree, push off the wide, bark-covered trunk, and rebound, soaring through the air, taking the hyena down by the head.

Blood sprays the forest floor as Brant's bear comes to join the fun. He picks up the dazed hyena and slams him against the tree, bear-stomping him beneath his massive paws. I'd say our grizzly hasn't worked off all his pent-up hostility after his river trip, but honestly, this is how Brant fights on any day.

The coyote with the bum back leg is snarling and snapping the air in circles, trying to keep us away. The only way he survives this is by retreating and he knows it.

Brant barrels forward and knocks the second coyote into the tree. The crunch of bone precedes a pitiful yelp and then they drop their heads and concede. Brant lets off an ear-shattering roar and the two slink away to lick their wounds.

I head back to the others, but I don't need to hurry.

The battle is won, and Hawk is digging into the backpack to find our girl some more clothes. I don't mind that she can't flash clothing on like the rest of us. It gives us the chance to admire her in the raw at regular intervals.

"Is everyone good?" I ask joining them. "Brant's comin'. Where's our wolf?"

Hawk points off into the trees. "He and Keyla are running a perimeter to make sure we're clear."

"*Are* we clear?"

"I suspect not. That was a tracking party. My guess is there's a force on the other side of the river set up to ambush us at what they think is the actual portal gate site. They probably think we're sneaking in the long way."

"Little do they know." I smile. "Okay, so, let's check out this site and get gone before they realize we're not comin' over to their side."

Lukas gives us each a nod. "You guys take a moment. I'll grab Amir and Alex and scout ahead."

"Should they be running off ahead when we've been attacked," Calli asks. "Shouldn't we all stay together?"

Hawk smiles. "I think he's giving you a moment and some space to get dressed. Lukas has lived among wildlings long enough to understand that when a female is vulnerable and naked, it's best to put some space between her and her mate… and in this case multiply that by four."

Calli looks surprised. "But it's Lukas and I'm naked around him more often than not."

Hawk chuckles. "Yes, it is and yes, you are. Still, he's being considerate and taking the others out of our path."

Kotah and Keyla return from their sweep in the trees.

Keyla heads over to check in with Doc and Kotah trots over to us, his tongue wagging out the side of his mouth once again. If anyone saw him like this, they'd never believe he's the same, stiff and somber male who was crowned twenty-four hours ago.

"Hey, Wolf. Thanks for the early warnin'. Are we all clear?" I run my fingers past the coarse guard hairs of his fur into the velvety coat underneath. He's stunning and majestic, his chocolate brown and silver coat so unique and striking, just like the man himself.

Kotah's nose is high and his head cants to the side as he sniffs the air.

My cat surges forward and I scan the surroundings. "What is it, my man? Have we still got hostiles?"

He shakes his head and moves to Calli.

"Hey, sweet prince," Calli says, tugging her shirt down over a pair of leggings. She rubs a hand over his head and caresses his velvety ears. She drops to one knee and meets him nose to nose. "What's up?"

He nuzzles into her neck and then draws his tongue up the side of her face.

Her squeal is filled with amusement as she wipes the wolf slobber off her chin. "Thanks for that. Goofball. I love you too."

As Calli giggles and trots off to meet up with Lukas further ahead, Kotah flashes back and stares at us, grinning.

"What's the look, Wolf?" Hawk asks.

Brant lumbers back and shifts to walk with us. "I

heard Calli squeal. What did I miss?"

I point to Kotah's grin. "To be determined. Go ahead, Wolf. Spill the beans."

Kotah chuckles. "When I caught Calli's scent, I figured out what the lore of the pendant means. I'll bet her full powers will be unlocked any time now."

Hawk's brow creases. "Would you mind cluing the rest of us in on your little epiphany?"

"When five become one, the power will be undone. The five of us *have* become one—a very tiny, precious one—our mate is pregnant."

My cat roars to the fore as my heart pounds at the inside of my ribcage. Is that what I've been sensing? The exhaustion. The niggle of something I'm missing? Before my emotions get ahead of me, I grip Kotah by the shoulders and take a breath. "You're sure?"

"Oh, yes. I'm sure." His grin nearly does me in. I grab those chiseled cheekbones and pull him in for a PDA like never before.

Hawk and Brant are chuckling somewhere close by, but I don't care. I'm having a baby. *We* are having a baby. I release Kotah and move to Brant, giving him a back-slapping bear hug and a kiss before moving on to Hawk.

The avian is looking at me like I've lost my mind—maybe I have—but I don't care.

"She's havin' our baby," I say, the forest spinning. "Shit, I need to sit down."

Hawk catches me as I list to the side. With his arms around me, I try to pull myself together. "Our baby."

He kisses my temple and steadies me on my feet.

"Yes, Jaguar. Our baby. A little kitten for us to love."

I think about that and them and everything this new life has given me and yeah… this is it.

It doesn't get any better than this. "Check please, my life is perfect."

CHAPTER ELEVEN

Brant

Five become one. Hells yeah, we did. Calli's carrying my cub and I'll be damned if Hawk's nightmare of a father will be shooting at her ever again. I don't give two shits if Calli thinks I'm the most overbearing Guardian of the Phoenix in mating history, the safety and well-being of both her and my young are the priority.

"What's with you guys?" Calli says, casting us a sideways glance. "All the doe-eyed glances and goofy grins are freaking me out a little."

"Just lovin' you, kitten," Jaxx says, handing her a power bar and water from Hawk's bag. "We finished another skirmish, how about you power-up and get hydrated?"

Calli giggles. "Thanks, puss. I could eat. And yeah, it can't hurt to have a few extra calories after that tussle, right?"

"Right you are," he says, grinning as she takes a bite and chews. "And when we get back to the plane, I'm callin' Mama and askin' her to make a feast when we get home."

"She doesn't need to do that. We can grab some drive-thru on the way to the airport."

"Drive-thru? Hells no. Home-cookin' is the way to go. It's much better for you. Besides, the last feast Mama made us ended well for all of us, didn't it?"

Calli flushes and checks that no one else is within earshot. "Okay, yeah, you boys making me your buffet table is probably *the* hottest moment in my sex life."

"Mine too," Jaxx and I say.

"Without a doubt," Kotah says.

"By a long-shot," Hawk says.

The avian says we can't risk telling Calli about the baby until we're clear of this forest and out of harm's way. He doesn't want her freaking out about being a mother when we have a task ahead and need our heads clear and in the game.

The ship has sailed on that one for Jaxx. The jaguar has seriously lost his mind. Then again, he's the only one of us who grew up with family and joyous kid memories and loving his parents. He knows how things can be.

The rest of us will have to figure it out on the fly.

I'm walking with Lukas when he gets the private message from Hawk. We might not be telling Calli yet, but Hawk thought Lukas should know so he has all the deets and will understand that our focus is securing her, now more than ever.

He pulls out his phone, reads the news, and then meets Hawk's crooked smirk with a genuine smile of his own.

Calli misses the entire exchange, engaged as she is with Jaxx, her power bar, and Kotah has shifted back to wolf and is zigzagging through the trees in front of her.

I chuckle. How can one tiny bit of news shift our worlds so massively that we went from being a devoted quint out to save the world to four dads determined to get out of this forest without anyone coming near our girl and our cub?

My FCO watch vibrates against my wrist and I glance to see what the message is. Oh. We're here. It's the coordinates tracker. "Okay, people, if Hawk's calculations are correct, this is where we need to be. On your toes. The old portal site should be right here somewhere."

The group fans out to look around and Kotah and Keyla circle back. When they join the search, the two of them shift back to human to help us look.

"The trees are smaller and thinner here than the forested area we've been traipsing through," Calli says.

"Ten years of growth instead of a lifetime," Kotah agrees. "On the original surveys, the land in question looked clear. Whoever did this took care to have the changes blend into the current forest. But look, if you know what you're looking for, you can see the line of the original riverbank."

We follow the trajectory of Kotah's pointed finger and yeah, he's right. The trees are bigger and thicker beyond a dip in the land. "Not only has the river been diverted, but the old path has been filled in."

We meander around the area and explore, searching for some sign of an ancient portal site.

Eventually, Lukas turns to Calli. "Do you feel anything? You could sense the fae energy at the Kansas site. Anything tweaking your radar here?"

Calli continues to wander through the maze of trunks and logs and scrub and stops next to a giant hemlock. The thing is massive. It stretches a hundred feet into the air and its trunk is an easy twenty-five feet wide. "This will sound crazy, but I don't think this tree is really here."

Lukas and Hawk move in and start palming the rough bark of the trunk.

Kotah leans in and sniffs the tree all the way around the back and returns on the other side. Even as a man, his sense of smell is probably better than any of ours.

Standing with his palms against the tree and his nose close to the wood. "I agree with Calli. This tree smells like magic, not nature."

Hawk leans in and sniffs things too. "And I recognize that smell. Where…" He stiffens and spins to assess our surroundings. "On your toes, boys."

Everyone tenses and we're all searching the trees now.

"What is it?" Calli asks.

"I recognize the scent of that magic. I've come across it more than once. It carries the signature of the Forest Lord."

My bear growls and pushes to the fore. "You mean the walking elk-tree abomination that nearly killed me?"

"Yeah, him," Hawk says, blanking out as he slips into one of his mental musings.

Jaxx frowns. "I see the hamster runnin' in your wheel, hotness. Would you like to share it with the rest of the class?"

"It makes sense if you think about it," Hawk says, his ebony brow creased deeply. "Greater Fae magic established the portal gates in the first place, right?"

Kotah nods. "Yes, that's right."

"And this entire area is heavily forested and wild."

"Agreed."

He runs a hand over the back of his neck and frowns. "I've been wondering for weeks how an ancient Forest Lord of the Fae Realm could live within the Human Realm for centuries and no one know or sense that level of magic."

There's no stopping my bear's growl as it rumbles from my chest. "You think the Forest Lord lives in this forest?"

"More than that," Kotah says. "You think he moved the river to protect the magic of the gate."

Hawk meets Kotah's gaze and shrugs. "I'm saying it's possible. Am I crazy or does that make sense in a convoluted sorta way?"

I chuff. "But why would he protect the gate when he's working against us. He nearly killed me when we raided the Black Knight compound and rescued those kids."

Hawk frowns. "Did he though? When we faced him, he wasn't in it to win it. He defended himself and then bugged out when things got heated."

"Yeah, you said that from the get-go," Jaxx says. "You thought he was being coerced or exploited somehow."

"I did and I *do*. I never understood how he got pulled into this, but if he is being forced to comply, he might not want my father to win. What if he was able to create a loophole and give us the chance to slip in and do what we need to do."

"Bullshit. That's a stretch," I grunt, my bear growling. "You're suggesting that your father strong-armed a mighty Forest Lord who somehow, ten years ago, had the foresight to move the land boundaries so he could control a dismantled portal gate?"

Hawk frowns. "I'm saying it's possible. Play along with me a little, will you, Bear? Not everything is black and white. There isn't always a truly good guy and a mustache-twirling bad guy. Sometimes there are shades of gray."

"The only shades of gray that interest me are those Fifty Shades that took the human world by storm. Other than that, I prefer the black and white model."

"That's narrow-minded and simplistic."

"Maybe I see things differently because I was the one getting pummeled and beaten with my bear brethren. If a Forest Lord is so all-fucking-powerful, how would he come under the control of your father? He's nothing but a fucking avian with money and a thirst for power."

The words are still burning like bile in my throat when I see them strike home. Hawk stiffens. "That description sounds familiar and awfully specific. Are you sure we're still talking about my father?"

I curse and take a step to close the distance. "I'm a mouthy asshole. Don't make it more than that. Yes, I was absolutely talking about your father. You and I are in a better place now. Don't let me fuck that up by spouting off."

Kotah moves in and grips Hawk's arm. "Brant is touchy about the Forest Lord because of his pain. His words came out wrong. Deep down, you know that."

I fist my hands at my sides and exhale. "Kotah's right, Hawk. I'm sorry. My mouth got ahead of me there. That's all it was. I swear."

Hawk stares at me a long moment before he nods. His frame is still rigid, but at least he unclenches his jaw. "I understand your frustration, Bear, and I accept your apology. If, however, there's more to it, I'd prefer you and I talk it out rather than have you harboring negative feelings and pretending we're all good."

I reach forward and clasp his hand in mine. "No pretending necessary. Seriously. We *are* all good."

When the tension subsides, we're all left standing in front of the tree that, according to Calli is not really there.

Hawk tips his head back and studies the trunk. "Back to the Forest Lord theory. If this is his work, it's Greater Fae magic and is above our pay grade."

Kotah breathes deeply and frowns. "Why do you think he'd be invested in the portal gate?"

"Maybe he's hoping to open it and get home. Maybe he's separated from someone he cares about. Forest Lords live a long time. It's plausible that he has a mate or a child in the Fae Realm."

Despite my bear's stubborn desire to stomp and shake my head, I have to give him that one. "Okay, that makes sense. If I was an immortal stranded here alone for ages, ten years would be nothing if I had a plan to get home."

Hawk reaches over and squeezes my wrist. "I honestly think this makes more sense than him working for my father by choice. The man is a master manipulator. He's forced him somehow."

Calli

While the boys hash out the who's and why's of what we're facing, I remain distracted by the illusion of what is real and not about this giant hemlock tree. It looks real. It feels strong and solid when I touch it, but something inside me recognizes that it's not what it appears.

Of all of us, I'm the noob when it comes to magic, so why is it me who can sense the glamor?

Is it a destiny thing?

Is it a Phoenix thing?

I close my eyes and focus on Riley. If my theory about contacting her through points where the veil between realms was or is weaker, maybe she can hear me if this portal gate isn't totally locked down.

If Hawk's right and the Forest Lord tried to safeguard the gate to give us an opportunity, maybe he's managed to pry the door open a crack.

Riley? Are you there? We're here now, on the other side of the gate I told you about. Any chance you're around?

I wait, my hopes diminishing with each passing moment that nothing comes back to me.

Riley... hellooooo. Anybody home?

Nothing. I exhale and get my head back in the game.

"If this is a glamor or an illusion, how do we take it down so we can see under the hood?"

Lukas studies the massive hardwood and frowns. "I'll give it a shot, but I have a feeling this is more about you than me doing my thing."

Maybe.

I'm watching Lukas do his mage magic thing when Jaxx and Brant both grip my shoulders and shuffle me back a few yards. "Better safe than sorry, kitten," Jaxx says.

Brant chuckles. "Yeah, you never can tell when our destiny might explode in our faces."

Kotah and Hawk join us and Kotah pulls his mating crystal out from under his shirt. "I've got an idea about the Guardian pendant," Kotah says, giving the guys a veiled smile. "The five become one part is complete, we know that."

The four of them share a private look.

"Yeah, we do," Jaxx says, winking at me and grinning ear to ear.

"And we all touched and completed the circuit in the truck, but the point of the Guardians of the Phoenix was that the four strongest wildling representatives guard the phoenix. What if we must be in our wildling forms and touching to trigger the unlocking. Maybe the five become one part only sets the stage."

"It can't hurt to try." I squeeze Kotah's arm and smile. "Good thinking, sweet prince. Do you want me to shift?"

The guys look hesitant about that for some reason.

Kotah waves them off. "Yes. It's fine. Let's shift."

I'm not sure what's going on with them, but I'm sure they'll sort themselves out. I take a step back, toe off my shoes, and set them safely on a fallen log. Thanks to the last ambush, I'm down to one pair of shoes. Hawk brought several outfits but only one extra pair of shoes.

Next, I work on removing my clothes. When I turn back around, I have a jaguar, a bear, a wolf, and a hawk all sitting in a row watching me take off my clothes.

"Seriously? You boys get off on cheap thrills. If I could flash into my phoenix without ruining my clothes, I would. Why torch a perfectly good outfit without reason, amirite?"

Once I'm bare to the natural world, I check the height clearance and move to a spot a few feet away. Now that my mythological beast side and I are friends, it takes only the slightest thought to call my phoenix forward.

One minute, I'm an average-sized, slightly chesty blonde and the next, I'm a fifteen-foot mythical firebird with a thirty-foot wingspan of gold and copper flames.

It's so freaking awesome.

Hawk hops off the forest floor and lands on Brant's back and then Jaxx pushes in on the bear's right shoulder and Kotah rubs against his left. When they're all huddled in, I take a beat to stare at them and sigh.

Sooo freaking awesome.

No matter how fearsome they are, they'll always be my personal fur babies. I finish taking a mental screenshot and then step closer, reaching around the four of them with my wings and encircling them in my hold.

The moment my fiery feathers brush over their fur

and feathers, magic bursts free. The rush of power steals my breath. It overloads my cells with sensation and light and energy all at once.

The forest spins and I focus on the giant hemlock to keep from swooning. Whatever I am meant to become it's happening—right now.

Fae magic explodes from within me.

It's hot and wild and seems endless as my cells ignite and my phoenix feeds on the sudden influx of power. I lift my beak into the air and let off a shrill screech as I'm lifted off the forest floor and suspended in a vortex of fire.

Despite not knowing what's happening, I'm not afraid.

Everything is as it's supposed to be.

I feel that deep inside my soul. I am exactly where I am meant to be, with the men I am meant to be with, and we're about to open the gate.

Shifting my gaze from my mates below to where Lukas is standing next to the massive hemlock tree, I see through the veil of magic to what lays beneath. It's a seam in the fabric of our realm. A fissure sealed. A scar healed.

But it's a seam none the less.

And with the influx of power comes a new understanding of what I must do. *Change back, boys. It's time for the mating crystals to unite.*

I'm not sure how I know to communicate with them through the new mental wavelength, but I feel it. Like I felt them physically strengthening on the mating bond from the beginning, I feel them mentally now too.

The four of them return to their human forms and yep, their crystals are glowing.

Wrap them together. They're ready now.

Hawk does what I ask and shouts as the four shards make contact. He tosses the bundle, but it doesn't fall. It rises in the air, hovering like some alien entity in a movie.

Fused together, the four shards throw off a burst of light and energy like a small sun going supernova.

My mates shield their eyes, but I don't need to. This fire is part of me. The supernova rises in the air and as it grows closer, it throws off the swirling colors each of the shards did as they awarded themselves to my guardians: silver, blue, gold, green, purple.

It's a kaleidoscope of raw energy and it's free at last.

Instead of coming to me, as I expect, the pulsing supernova hovers in the air, right in front of the sealed seam. My way is clear. I remember the cave paintings Kotah showed me that sunny afternoon in the grotto. The image had me hovering and blowing fire, creating the link between realms.

I breathe deep and blow a stream of fire onto the crystals.

As the crystals grow hotter, the power within vibrates and expands. The potential energy is building and tingles at the nape of my neck.

Opening a gateway between two worlds will take a huge amount of energy. I continue to heat the crystals and the seam of the sealed gate starts to shimmer.

The portal gate is opening again. I know it is. I feel

it.

"Incoming," Hawk shouts.

I look down to the forest floor, just as the entire area breaks into the battle of a warzone.

"No, Spitfire. Keep going."

I'm torn. My mates are scrambling but this is everything we've worked for. Deciding to trust them to keep themselves safe, I return my focus to the little sun of power I've created.

This is my destiny.

This is what the past three months were about.

I take another breath and keep at it.

Gunfire echoes through the trees. Wildlings shift and their promise of violence permeates the forest. Magic snaps and expands as our war with the minions of the Black Knight explodes all around me.

The crystals are humming—the sound they give off a high-pitched whistle. It's like the boiling of a kettle and I need to push it until it blows.

I breathe another breath and blow more fire.

Men in the forest below face off against me, emptying their automatic weapons but nothing penetrates the heat of my flaming form.

The whistle of the crystals becomes a scream and I smile as the colors are drowned out by the white-hot light. Something is about to happen. Something forceful and important.

Another breath and more fire.

The explosion is deafening.

I shriek as the air ignites with astonishing pressure.

My wings are extended, and the rush catches me unprepared. I'm knocked backward, toppling through the air. The forest spins in a green blur as I'm thrown from my orbit and crash into the trees. I blink, trying to focus on the pulsing surge of power.

I flame out, my phoenix form lost, my energy spent.

Hopefully, someone else knows what to do next because I've got nothing left.

The world comes crashing in on me as Black Knight militia moves in. The first bullet snaps my shoulder back, the second shatters my knee...

The shouts of my mates are drowned out by the blood rushing in my head. As the world goes dark, I'm content in the knowledge that we did it.

My destiny is fulfilled.

Whatever comes now is of secondary importance.

The portal gate is open.

CHAPTER TWELVE

Jaxx

Calli is blown backward like a flaming pinwheel until she crashes into a cluster of trees. She hits hard and I let off a roar. The four of us launch to get to her, my cat wild with panic and fury. Calli is down and she's taking fire. She's no longer flamed up and bulletproof—and she's taking fire.

There's no thought or emotion in me. My entire being is driven by primal instinct. These motherfuckers are trying to take what is mine. My mate. My love. My baby.

They dare to stalk her. To fire on her.

Brant is the first to get there and is shredding people left and right. Still, no matter how fast I run, on two feet or four, there's no way I'll get to her in time to intercept the men moving in. My heart shatters.

How can we lose her now?

Kotah and Keyla launch through the air, tearing at men and taking them down. There are just too many of them.

If they're here to stop us from opening the portal

they're too late. Calli did it. It's a waste of life to keep fighting now. Hawk takes flight and closes the distance. He'll get to her, but we all sense the trauma of what's happened.

Calli's pain vibrated across our mating bond before she lost consciousness. She's hurt… really hurt.

I make it into the scrum as another surge of magic bursts beside us and the Forest Lord appears. Brant goes berserker but before he gets close enough to attack, the giant tree man leans down, touches Calli, and the two of them disappear.

"No!" Hawk screams. "Bring her back!"

I stare at the empty space and horror throbs in my veins. I let my cat take full ascension and a deadly calm falls over me.

They will die for this.

Hawk

The floor of my stomach drops the moment Calli disappears and the forest goes out of focus. He took her. I defended him. I thought he might've been coerced… and he took her.

My mind flushes hot and I'm stunned.

"Never let the world see what matters to you, son. It only empowers people to hurt you." The words trigger a memory of the worst kind and cold dread grips my bowels.

Frozen in place, I look for the man who spoke them.

The moment my father exits the trees, my insides recoil.

He's here. After all the years I fought to forget him and leave his cruelty behind, the moment I see him, I'm a ten-year-old boy watching him strangle my pet rabbit.

"Hawks eat rabbits, son. We don't make friends with them," he said. "So let's cook him up and have supper."

He ignored my pleas, grabbed my wrist, and pulled me along behind him toward the house. "Never let the world see what matters to you, son. It only empowers people to hurt you. Today you'll learn a lesson and fill your stomach at the same time."

"Hello, Sabastian," he says raking me with an icy smile. "Why the long face. Misplaced someone, have you?"

"If you harm one hair on her head, I'll kill you where you stand, old man."

My father laughs. "Oh, you always did have delusions of grandeur. You can't touch me. Never could."

I try to swallow, but my throat is locked. He's here. After everything he's done to me, to my company, to my mates… he's here and he's smiling and he walked out of the fucking trees like he's the fucking king of the world.

And he's laughing that he has Calli.

The world stops.

Bang. Bang. Bang. Bang.

Shots ring out and I watch scarlet circles appear where a moment ago there were none. While my gaze remains locked on my father as he crumples to the forest floor, the firefight continues around me.

What does it matter? Calli's gone. My father's dead.

Why are his fucking minions still fighting?

I don't know how long it takes until the sounds of battle cease. Maybe it's a minute or maybe it's ten. In the end, all eyes turn on me.

"Give Lukas the gun, hotness," Jaxx says, turning my head to look at him.

I'm lost in a daze and then I look down and see Lukas disarming me, my arm still up and poised to fire. "Did I kill my father?"

"No one blames you," Brant says, sliding in against my side. "He had that coming and more."

I shake myself inwardly and straighten. "No argument, but personal closure aside, I shouldn't have done that. How will we find Calli?"

"We'll find her," Kotah says, squeezing my arm and releasing the anguish I feel over costing us information on Calli's whereabouts. "It's done. And we'll find her"

"Or not," my father says, rising from the ground. He brushes off the sleeves of his jacket and chuckles. "Points for coming at me head-on, son. I didn't think you had it in you."

"He didn't stay dead," I say, despite it being obvious.

"Did you think it would be that easy, Sabastian? I'm disappointed."

"Not living up to you is high praise. Glad to disappoint."

He casts me a crooked smile, but I see that my lack of respect irks him. "Honestly, your problem was always one of vision, son. You never did see past the next three moves of your opponent."

I scrub a hand over the spot where my aneurism is about to blow out of my skull. "Honestly, I bet if I behead you right now, you'd finally shut the fuck up. Now, where is my wife?"

Calli

I wake in what I can only describe as a thatched cavern. If it was made from rock, I'd call it a massive cave, but it's not. It's woven sticks with leaves and plants growing in a vast, living arboretum. And it's someone's home.

I'm lying naked and bloody on a massive bed, cushioned by a blanket of moss beneath me. My raw and brutalized state is a direct contrast to the serenity of the little home. There are books on bookshelves and lanterns lit to give us light and a bench and table seating area over by the far wall.

"Don't be afraid," a kid says from the shadows of the dark corner. "He won't hurt you—*we* won't hurt you."

I blink and try to sit up. It's too soon after being shot and I flop back to the pillow. My shoulder seems to have healed well enough, but my knee is still a mess.

"Where are we? How'd I get here?" I'm fighting the fog blanketing my mind and remember the battle. "You have to take me back."

"You're hurt and naked."

"I'll heal and naked is nothing new."

"I don't think we have anything you can put on to cover yourself. Sorry. My t-shirts won't fit and he doesn't wear any. A blanket maybe?"

I wave that away. "Fabric burns until my skin cools. I don't suppose you have a fire blanket or anything flame resistant?"

"Sorry," the kid says. "Fresh out."

"I figured. Okay, what happened? Why bring me here when there's a battle being fought?"

The kid steps into the light and can't be more than thirteen. "Because people shot holes in you? Yeah, wow, you really are naked."

"Yep, sorry. Nothing to be done about it right now." I sit up and test my knee. It's a bit achy, but my healing has fully taken hold. And while that's good news, the tilt-a-whirl going on in my head isn't. "I need to eat. It's been a draining day and if I don't eat, I'll collapse."

The boy looks across the grassy floor. "I've got cold pizza leftover from last night. You want a couple of slices?"

"Perfect, thanks. So, if we're close enough to get pizza, do you think we can get out of here and find our way back to where I was in Pennsylvania?"

He shakes his head and comes back with the cardboard box. "No. Rowan and I are both travelers. The pizza place isn't close. I just pop to anyplace and get what we want. I do know we're in Alaska, though, and that's way beyond my range. Your best chance of getting back to Pennsylvania anytime soon is to wait until Rowan returns."

I'm chewing my first slice of cold, meat-lover's when I recognize the boy. "Yarko?"

He frowns and backs away. "Yeah. Who are you? How do you know me?"

My heart picks up and I scootch to the edge of the bed. "I don't know you personally, but Brant Robbins is one of my mates. I recognize you from the pictures he had while we were searching for you last month. He's an FCO Enforcer, big guy, brown wavy hair, always cracking wise."

He seems appeased by that answer and nods. "Yeah. I know him. Brant's cool."

"He is. He worked tirelessly to find you kids and get you rescued and returned to life. It tore him up inside when you ran away."

Yarko shrugs. "Leaving wasn't about him. While I was being held by Sabastian and his men, my parents died in a car crash. There was no one for me to go home to, so I found my own home with Rowan. People are scared of him but he's nice. He watched out for us when Sabastian made us do things we didn't want to do. He kept us safe."

It sounds like Hawk was right about him… or at least, partially. "I appreciate the save, I do, but I need to get back. My mates were in the middle of a fight to the death and will be losing their shit right now not knowing where I am."

The hair on my nape prickles and I tense as magic snaps in the air. Rowan the Forest Lord is back. He appears across the room and I sense immediately that the distance is for my benefit.

"Wow. You are much bigger and scarier up close."

He holds out his hands in a gesture I assume is supposed to feel less threatening. It doesn't work, but I appreciate it. "I am pleased you are well, Phoenix. It's time to end this. Come. I must take you back before Sabastian gets away with his evils and I lose my chance. Hurry."

I open my mouth to argue, but a moment ago I was asking to be taken back. Leap of faith time. He did, after all, give me a time out while I healed instead of allowing Sabastian's men to swiss cheese me.

I offer him my hand and the moment we touch, I'm back in the forest, standing next to the pulsing rift between realms that I created.

The carnage strewn across the forest floor is mind-boggling. I stare, trying to make sense of it. Corpses litter the forest floor, throats torn out, chest cavities cracked wide, and blood saturating the earth beneath.

I've never been squeamish, but gross.

Yarko doesn't seem all that bothered. That's disturbing in itself. What exactly did Sabastian have him doing?

As my blood-covered mates turn to look at me, I point to the devastation. "I am *not* helping you clean that up."

"Spitfire." Hawk turns away from—

"Oh my, you caught your father."

He ignores my surprise and tromps through the death pile to get to me. "Thank fuck you're alright. We thought you…" He looks up at Rowan and his gaze hardens. "Why did you take her?"

"Men were shooting her, and she was defenseless. I gave her time to heal and brought her back—"

The violent rumble of Brant's bear precedes him baring down on Rowan in a four-legged grizzly fury. He's either going to kill Rowan or die trying. "Brant, stop! He helped me."

My words fall on deaf ears.

Brant, stop! I shout at him through the link of our

unspoken conversation. *He saved me. He kept me safe so I could heal. He protected Yarko too. Look your missing kid is here.*

Something in that gets through and his rampage of rage slows. Damn, he's a macabre mess. His fur is caked and matted with blood. Did he battle to survive or put Sabastian's men through a woodchipper?

"Hey, big guy," I say, forcing a smile. "Don't kill the ancient tree man, okay. Hawk's right, there's more to this than we know."

My bear shakes his broad, boxy head and lifts his black nose into the air. He lets off a baleful cry and I feel the weight of his anguish across the mating bond. "You thought he hurt me like he hurt you and your friends. He didn't. Stand down and let's find out what's going on."

I make the request and wait, unsure he'll listen.

He seems to consider it, eyeing up the huge barky tree creature in our midst, and then his muscled shoulders lock tight, and he stops snarling.

I exhale a breath I didn't realize I was holding. "Thanks, Bear. Okay, how about you all hit the river and get washed up, and then we'll see what we can about what's been going on? And does anyone know where my clothes are?"

Keyla rushes them over and I make quick work of pulling pants up my thighs and tugging a sweater over my head. Damn. In three months, I've destroyed more underwear than I care to think about.

My four mates haven't moved, and I look over to Lukas and the FCO guys. "You've got us covered, right boys? My mates are okay to step away for two minutes to get less disgusting?"

Lukas tests the bindings holding Sabastian and nods. "Yeah. Go ahead. If he tries anything, I'll shoot him full of holes. By the time you all get back he'll be getting up, but you'll hear the shots and know to come back."

Hawk smiles. "Good plan. And remember what I said about decapitating him. I think it's the way to go."

Lukas's mouth quirks up at the side. "I'll take it under advisement."

Kotah, Brant, and Hawk each pass by me, give me a quick hug and kiss, and head to the river. Jaxx's jaguar circles my feet growling and lays down on all fours like an Egyptian Sphinx, glaring out at the world.

"I'm okay, puss. If you want to get cleaned up, I promise I won't get shot or kidnapped while you're gone."

Jaxx simply growls louder.

"Okay then," I say, looking up to everyone else. "I can't argue with that."

Hawk

Kotah, Brant, and I wash up quickly in the icy waters of the river and head back. Brant and Kotah fought in their wildling forms, so their clothes aren't stained with blood. I can't say the same. I am most comfortable fighting as a man and am regretting not packing a change of clothes for myself.

I don't want the blood of our kills anywhere near Calli... or our baby.

I sigh. Poor Jaxx. When Calli was taken, he lost himself more than I've ever seen. He's our strong and steady. Our laughter. Our Passion.

I twist the wide, platinum mating band on my finger and my heart aches for him. He thought we lost her... them.

By the time we get back, Calli and the kid are building a fire, The FCO guys are guarding my father where he's bound to a tree with magic, and Keyla, Doc, and Lukas are working with the Forest Lord, creating a clearing for the portal gate.

The fact that in the five minutes we've been gone there's already a fifty-foot square clearing proves how much power the Rowan possesses. And really… he's a Forest Lord. It makes sense that he'd have domain over the trees of a forest.

"Well, this will make securing the site and building a gatehouse easier," Kotah says.

"Much," I say, pulling my phone from my pocket. "Good afternoon, Jayne. Update time."

I fill her in on the unfolding events, relay our location, ask for a supply drop of materials and camping gear, and let her know that despite unloading my gun into my father, the spawn of evil still lives.

"I've never known you to be a quitter, Barron. If at first you don't succeed…" she says.

I chuckle. "Oh, I'll try again real soon, I'm sure."

"Do you think your mother might have taught him a trick or two to tether his life somehow?"

"Not sure, but I'll talk to Lukas about it. Don't worry. We'll figure out how to put the mangy dog down."

"Okay, I'm dispatching what you asked for to secure

the site. You'll have reinforcements and supplies in under four hours."

I check my watch and set a timer. "Good. That's it for now." I hang up and tuck my phone away.

"Are we good?" Brant asks.

"We will be in a few hours. Until then, we rough it."

Yarko looks up as we join him, Calli, and Jaxx by the fire. He smiles and points to the flames. "With her around, we didn't even need matches."

Brant's still shakier than he's letting on, but he nods. "She's a marvel our phoenix. There's no question."

The three of us make our attempt at appearing nonchalant as we settle next to our mate, but there's no getting around it. Our animal sides are pacing and need reassurance that Calli is whole. We watched her get shot and then kidnapped and were unable to help her.

Wolf, can you still smell the baby? Is everything okay?

The dip in his chin is almost imperceptible, but that subtle affirmation sears my heart with relief. "Thank fuck."

Calli blinks up at me and smiles. "Watch out, broody man, we have impressionable ears listening."

She gestures to Yarko but the kid doesn't seem the slightest bit put off by my language.

Still, with a baby on the way, I might as well start trying to curb my colorful vocabulary. I want to set a good example.

As the crackle of flames builds in the air, the scent of woodsmoke fills our nostrils. I sit next to Calli and let my mind wander. The future is pregnant with possibilities.

A future that was almost taken from us twice today. I take Calli in my arms and hold her tight against my chest. *I love you, Spitfire. Are you fully recovered?*

Do you mean am I up for a tryst in the forest to reassure your wildling side?

I chuckle. *Something like that.*

Other than being highly inappropriate with our current traveling companions, your father as our prisoner, and unresolved destiny issues, I'm totes there.

I press my lips against her neck and breathe her in. *And if I figure all that out?*

She laughs and flashes me a skeptical grin. *If you figure all that out, consider me naked and willing.*

Challenge accepted. Never underestimate a male's need to be inside his mate.

Kotah steps in closer and frowns. "I sense your hunger, *Chigua.* Are you well? That was a lot of energy to expend."

She offers him a sweet smile. "I'm okay, but yeah, I could eat. I don't know why I've been so hungry lately."

Brant heads over to where our backpacks are, and I take a mental inventory of what we've each eaten over the day. "I'm not sure what food is left. I packed for an afternoon on the river and a hike, not for an all-day event."

And at the time, I didn't know my mate was pregnant.

Kotah shrugs. "We certainly can keep everyone fed. We have a fire to cook and the forest holds everything we need to survive."

Calli chuckles. "You make it sound like we're getting ready to camp out. We opened the portal gate. Aren't we heading back to civilization?"

I shake my head. "Sorry, Spitfire. Not anytime soon, I'm afraid. Opening the rift is only the first step. Now we have to secure this site and ready for the next phase."

Her gaze narrows on us. "And what's the next phase?"

"To reestablish the portal gate, we have to build a bridge between the realms."

"Oh, right. Of course."

"And then secure it so we can regulate who travels back and forth."

"And there's the issue of the Forest Lord," Kotah says. "Did you find out what your father is holding over him?"

I nod. "When the portal gates closed so suddenly, he was separated from his clan and left behind. The fire dervishes took him in, and he married one of the elders. Part of his pledge was to guard them and their forest until he's able to return home. About six months ago, my father came here to check the portal gate sites. There were altercations and he and his men took the fire dervish elder council hostage."

"A real peach, your old man," Calli says.

"Isn't he though?"

Kotah toes the dirt and frowns. "So, Rowan feels duty-bound to rescue them. Why can't he do it himself?"

"He says they're being held in the middle of a human population and my father has set up magic dampeners. He's powerless to glamor himself from the narys or storm the castle and kick ass."

Calli nods. "People would notice an eight-foot magical tree walking around."

"Exactly. He needs a team that can blend. At first, he had access to the empowered kids. He was gaining their trust, but then we rescued them and took that option off the table."

"And now his sights are on us?"

"He knew the phoenix was destined to open the portal gate so he helped us so we'd help him."

Calli shrugs. "I have no problem getting prisoners back from your father's clutches. If he knows where they are, I say we do it."

That's my girl.

A warrior always ready to take on the big bad wolves of the world. Or, in this case… the big bad hawk. "I told him we'd help him, but I needed to check on you and your state of fitness first."

Brant jogs back and pulls out half a sandwich. "It's a little squished but it'll taste the same."

The alpha in me hates the fact that my mate is hungry and forced to eat damaged food, but Brant's right, it'll serve its purpose until we can get more.

"Hey, Wolf, could run us down a couple of rabbits?"

Kotah's entire demeanor brightens. "Hunt, to feed my mate? It would be my greatest honor."

"Oh, count me in," Keyla says, joining us. "It's been years since we hunted together and yeah, I could eat."

Kotah offers his sister a content smile before kissing Calli and jogging off. "Prepare the spit. We'll be back shortly."

CHAPTER THIRTEEN

Kotah

Keyla and I shift on the fly and race into the trees. Today has been quite a day. I spent hours with my nose to the ground and my claws tearing into the pithy soil of the forest floor. The scents are home to me and the fresh air fills my lungs with every inhale. It's heaven.

Then, there are all the blessings of the day: the baby, Calli opening the rift between realms, our full powers being unlocked, our new telepathic link, her returning to us unharmed… it's been a day to remember.

Keyla veers to the right and her full, white coat catches the breeze. Her wolf has always been breathtakingly beautiful, but when she's on a hunt there is a joy that makes her even more stunning.

I follow her lead and soon catch the scent that set her on her path. The rabbit isn't far ahead of us and we'll soon be upon it. I let her take the lead and watch as she navigates the uneven ground. Her joy feeds my soul and I'm thankful, now that I'm back in her everyday life, and that she reconnected to the girl I grew up with.

I think about my mother sitting in her stuffy gown perched stiffly on the edge of her seat at my coronation.

What will she do when we get her back? She's no longer in power. Some people are defined by what they do and how people see them. My mother is one of them.

Without that, she's a shell of a person.

Keyla is half a body length ahead of me and scares up the rabbit, shifting her footing without missing a beat. We dodge left and I allow the pull of the hunt to draw my wolf to the fore. The moment he's fully engaged my instincts kick in with a warning.

We are not alone.

Calli

I finish the squished sandwich and am thankful for it. Still, it doesn't begin to fill the hollow pit that is now my stomach. I feel like Pippin in Lord of the Rings. What about second breakfast? Elevenses? Luncheon? Afternoon tea? Dinner? Supper? Man, I'm beginning to sound as bad as Brant.

Brant and Yarko are busy gathering sticks and constructing the spit for the fire. I'm sure it won't be long until the next meal is served. Maybe the kid could pop out and grab us a dozen pizzas in the meantime.

Spitfire, how about you, Jaxx, and I take a walk to the river. I know how badly my wild side is raging and how much I want you, but Jaxx lost control of his cat when you were taken and he needs you. Despite propriety, I think the two of you need to take a moment.

I meet Hawk's gaze and smile. *And what will you be doing during my moment with Jaxx?*

Watching out for you.

Or watching us?

He chuckles. *Guilty as charged. That too. He's suffering though. I feel it.*

I hate the idea that any of my mates should suffer for something within my power to fix. And yeah, being with Jaxx is no hardship. When I stand, I try to find a spot on his coat that isn't gross, so I can touch him. "Come on, cowboy. Let's get you cleaned up."

Whether or not he's worried about the blood and death dried in his coat, my jaguar guardian rises to his paws and follows me across the little area we've cleared as our base camp. Walking hand in hand with Hawk, the three of us are just leaving the light of the fire when something massive shifts in the shadows.

"Crap, Rowan," I say, patting my chest. "You scared me, dude."

"I've been patient. I helped you five for a reason. I need your help in return."

Hawk nods. "And I haven't forgotten about you, but Calli must eat after a battle, or her phoenix flames out and she collapses. It's happened before and we almost lost her. It won't do anyone any good for us to venture off on the next quest and have her fall unconscious. The wolves are hunting now. We'll feed her and then be ready."

The greater fae tree straightens and meets us head-on. "If the boy and I bring food, will you then be able to help me?"

Hawk nods. "Yeah, food is our only issue. Calli needs to eat after a battle and she's had two today."

"Consider it done."

The huge tree stalks off toward the fire and I'm left

blinking up at Hawk. "Why do I feel like we're about to be buried in a mountain of pizza?"

Hawk makes a face and then tugs me toward the river once again. "If that's the case, we've got maybe twenty minutes before he's back."

Jaxx

The river is cold when I first step into the flow of the water but not for long. Calli strips off her clothes and wades in, and with her comes a rush of heat. She's like a living pool heater… a sexy, skinny dipping pool heater.

"That's it, puss. Let's get some of this carnage washed off. I like my men authentic and manly but covered in the blood of our enemy is a bit much."

Her hands feel wonderful as she cups water over my shoulders and scrubs her fingers through my fur. Bent over as she is, I get a lovely eyeful of her tits swaying near my face and Hawk's not complaining about getting the peeping Tom show of her naked ass.

Okay, yeah. Enough jaguar for one day, I want my mate. Holding off for some delayed gratification, I close my eyes and absorb her touch a little longer.

My willpower doesn't last long.

Calli gasps when I shift forms and take her in my arms. There's no time for chit-chat. I need her. Maybe I should've shifted sooner. "Sorry, kitten," I say, lifting her against my chest and splitting her legs, "all the southern gentleman is currently drained out of me."

I'm nothing but desire. Hunger. Need.

She wraps her arms around my neck and lets off a guttural groan as my cock slides inside her. "You do you, Jaxx."

And I do. Water laps around our naked bodies as I step deeper into the water and claim her mouth. I nip and play, showing her how delicious I think she is.

Kissing her fuels me. She tastes like smokey passion and I love it when my kisses draw out her wildcat. She hungers… and claws… and takes what she wants without apology.

I grip the back of her neck with one hand, the other trailing down her side to the fleshy round of her breast. My palm skims over the mound, teasing her nipple up to a tight peak.

She moans into my mouth, tangling her tongue around mine, and arching into my touch. There have been play sessions between sex where we've made out so hot and heavy one or both of us have orgasmed without even having sex.

Not this time. I'm thick and hard inside her, getting squeezed by her greedy core and there will be sex in this orgasm. I tweak her nipple between my thumb and forefinger, and she shudders, rocking against me.

Her unbridled response sends a shot of hot pleasure straight into my cock. "Hot damn, kitten," I groan. "I need you so bad."

Shifting us a few yards upstream, I find a deeper pool and a little ledge where I can play better under the surface. I feel the heat of Hawk's gaze and wish we were home and had the whole night to ourselves.

Thinking about adding in my mates, sends a thrilling burn radiating through me. "If you're gonna watch, hotness, come make yourself useful."

"You sure? This can be a couple's moment."

I pull back from Calli's kiss and the answer shines in her smoldering gaze. "Yeah, get naked and get in here. The water's fine and so's our mate."

"Yes, sir." The amusement in Hawk's tone eases my cat a little.

Now that I'm cock deep in my mate and can feel her energy surrounding me, things have shifted from mate anxiety to full hard-on lust. I circle my hips, thrusting and retreating, enjoying the whole hot tub effect of having a horny phoenix on my cock.

A moment later, Hawk is there and he's gloriously naked. "Damn, hotness. When you look at me with that cocky smirk, it makes me want to do bad things to you."

"Oh, that we had time. Sadly this is an appetizer, not a feast."

Right. "Okay then, quick and dirty it is. I claimed first position, but you go ahead and enjoy yourself doing whatever you think we have time to do." Leaving him with that, I go back to moving inside her.

Calli

Too much. How many times have I thought I could combust from the pleasure of having one or all of these men? Too many. Kissing Jaxx is the sweetest agony, the blissful decadence of his playful kitty while being sized up by the alpha predator to be consumed.

His arms are tight around me and he's plunged inside me to the hilt. Each time he brushes my clit, my sex throbs with a deeper need. How is that even possible?

I clutch him close, fighting the urge to release my wild side completely, while I buck against him.

Hawk closes in behind me and gathers my hair. Shifting it away from my neck, he drops his mouth to my bare shoulder and his breath washes over my skin. "So. Fucking. Hot."

I groan as he nuzzles and nips at my shoulder—the same shoulder Brant bit earlier today. His mark has healed, of course, but I still feel the erotic sting of his hold on me as Hawk's steel length presses hard against the small of my back. Hawk's tall… too tall to be inside me at the same time as Jaxx when we're standing. Jaxx picks up his rhythm and each penetration has me clamoring for more.

"That's what I'm talking about," Brant says, wading in to join us.

"So much for a discreet moment," Hawk chuckles against my neck.

"Hey, if you weren't having a party, you shouldn't have sent the sexy invitation over the mating bond."

I let my eyes roll closed as another set of hands caress my ass and down my arms. Yeah, I feel it then, our mating bond is lit up and throbbing with sexual need. I suppose that's as good as an invitation. All we need to make it perfect is—

"I'm here, *Chigua*," Kotah whispers softly against the shell of my ear.

"Good," I groan, my voice ragged. "So good—*oh!*"

Hawk tilts me back off Jaxx's chest and a rush of warm water flows over my skin. I open my eyes and catch Kotah's smile. He's watching the moonlight glisten on my wet breasts, my nipples standing straight up off my chest.

The growl of my wolf vibrates right to my core and I bite my lip to keep from crying out.

Hawk mutters something and I feel the tingle of magic fall over us. "No holding back, Spitfire. I dropped the cone of silence over us. A little gift from my mother's side."

"Thank gawd," I gasp, letting off a groan simply because I can. "More Jaxx. If no one can hear us, I want you to make me scream."

"Yes, ma'am."

"Hawk, raise her shoulders a little. Brant and Kotah, you've got her legs." Jaxx adjusts the angle of my hips and presses against a raw and delicious spot deep inside me.

"Oh, yes," I groan, my breath getting sucked from my lungs. "Right there."

Jaxx chuckles. "You say that like I don't know where all your sensitive spots are, kitten. We know you inside and out. Prepare to scream and cream."

"That's poetic, Jaguar," Brant says. "Prepare to scream and cream. I'm getting t-shirts made."

Jaxx's hips thrust forward and my vision fritzes. He rubs that spot again and it's like raw bliss. I do as instructed and close my eyes, absorbing every probing stroke. My head falls back to the surface of the water and I groan at the ecstasy of it all: Jaxx's cock, the touch of my mates, the warm water lapping at my skin as he picks up his pace and rocks harder and harder inside me.

With the four of them holding me, there's no fear of

sinking. I close my eyes again and absorb it. One important thing that blindfolded sex with Hawk has taught me is how much I love sensation.

Lost in the pumping thrusts, with my breasts being caressed, and the *slap, slap, slap* of water splashing against my skin, I embrace the keening building inside me.

Jaxx isn't the only one who needs this. We all do.

"Purr for me, Jaxx."

The throaty rumble of my jaguar does me in. He plunges into me a few more times and my body shatters. I'm lost to him, as I always am. I swallow and try to hold off, but with Jaxx's purr and his cock and his throaty grunts filling my ears, my hips convulse and my world shatters.

I cry out, arching in the water as my mates support me, and Jaxx's breathing hitches in a throaty grunt.

On a shout, he pitches his hips forward and locks into place. With bruising fingers at my hips, he throws his head back and comes hard. I open my eyes then, to watch his end. With his muscled chest heaving and the cords in his throat strained tight, he spills into me.

My Texas cowboy in all his glory.

After a moment, he settles, and I ride out the ebbing waves of pleasure. Despite the world awaiting our return, I refuse to rush this. "Thank you, puss."

He withdraws and I shiver with the loss of his heat. "No. Thank you, kitten."

The other three are looking equally moved and I chuckle. "I don't care if everyone in that camp knows what we're up to. Is anyone else having trouble with their wild sides? Because I'm happy to keep doing what we're doing until all my mates are sated.

"Since you're offering," Brant says, waggling his brow. "My bear could use a moment of your time. And when I say moment, I mean it. Fuck, Jaguar, that was hot. I'm not gonna last long."

CHAPTER FOURTEEN

Hawk

By the time we get back, the five of us have calmed our wild sides and are ready to eat. In truth, we'd been hungry most of the day but giving Calli all the food was a no-brainer. She's the one who collapses *annnd* she has our baby phoenix growing inside her.

Fuck. I never thought I'd get weak in the knees about a baby. I never wanted kids. I never liked kids. But this baby is ours. The five of us came together in passion and love and created life.

Five become one.

Yep, I'm completely absorbed. I'm also scared shitless.

"What the hell?" Brant grumbles as we break from the trees. "Did Uber Eats explode in this forest while we were fooling around?"

I look at the spread of food and blink. "Looks like it."

Not far from the fire, someone has set up a makeshift, sawhorse table and the surface is covered from end to end with food: pizza, egg rolls, pans of lasagna, quartered chickens, potato salad, cheese tray, veggie tray, dessert squares…

"We didn't know what kind of food Calli eats," Yarko says, jogging over to meet us. "I said we should find you and ask but Rowan said we definitely shouldn't. I knew you ate pizza before, so I thought we were good to start there. Then, we went with a broad selection and figured we'd get lucky somewhere. Oh, and Doc and Keyla cooked the rabbits you caught too. There's plenty for everyone."

"I see that." Calli pulls to the front of the group and rushes to the table. "And yes, this is perfection. Thank you, both."

Yarko shrugs and grabs a square of cheese as he walks along the table with us. "Honestly, we did it so you and your husbands will help Rowan save his family. They aren't his real family but they took him in and they're good to him. That can be family too, can't it?"

"It absolutely can," Brant says. "It's the only family I ever had and it's all you need."

"Same," Calli says, popping an eggroll into her mouth. "My friend Riley and I were on our own from the time we were maybe a year or two older than you. We had each other and that was enough."

Yarko nods. "That's what I thought. So, eat, get strong, and then, you can help us get his family back."

I make a heaping plate and make sure Calli is getting enough on hers. "Give us fifteen minutes and we're all his."

"Cool. Thanks. I'll tell him."

When the kid jogs off, I catch a glimpse of me as a young boy, alone in the world and making the best of my situation. I feel responsible for the kid. After all, my father stole his last moments with his parents before their deaths.

"It's nice that he has someone who understands his powers who can watch out for him," Calli says.

"I'm not sure a Forest Lord is the best role model, but if not, I'm sure I can find a foster home for him."

Brant scoops a heaping mound of lasagna on his plate and points the serving spoon at us. "It so happens I know a fabulous couple who specialize in fostering lost boys. Margo and Ben would take him in, and he could grow up with a real family and not stuck in the woods with a giant walking-stick."

"Something to think about for sure, but as we all know, families come in all sorts of packages. If they're happy and thriving, it's none of our business."

Once we all have our selections made, I gesture to the seats by the fire and head over to join the others. "Okay, everyone, eat up and then we'll regroup and get ready to repay our favor to Rowan."

"Which is bullshit," Brant snaps. "Our destiny is right here. Calli and the portal gate. Nowhere in any of the lore did it mention rescuing fire dervishes from your old man's clutches."

"Honestly, I'm with Brant on this one," Jaxx says. "I think Calli's been through enough for one day. If we have to go, fine, but she should stay here and guard the gate. It's her destiny and she could rest."

"Hey! You trying to get rid of me, puss? I thought

we said no more splitting up. I'm good. By the time I eat all this food and we get our plan sorted, I'll be one hundy percent. Why would you want to bench me?"

Jaxx pegs me with a questioning gaze and I shake my head. *No. Not a good idea.*

Calli scowls and waves her fork between Jaxx and me. "What's with you guys today? I've been catching strange glances and weird vibes all afternoon. What am I missing?"

"Nothing we need to get into at the moment," I say, finishing my plate. "Yes, there is something we need to tell you, but it's private and we'd rather do it when we're not surrounded by fae creatures, friends, and foes."

Her frown deepens. "But you're all okay? No one's sick or hurt, or anything terrible?"

I chuckle and offer her a genuine smile. "Nothing at all terrible, just private. We'll talk about it when we get back to the castle or settle somewhere for the—"

Lukas shouts as an explosion lights up the clearing.

Sparks light up the night sky as power sizzles in the air. By the source of the magical pyrotechnics, I know in an instant what's happening.

My father's men are making their move.

I curse, drop my plate, and launch into the fray.

Shit. Shit. Shit.

Without thinking, I draw my gun and head for the tree where my father was tied up. Two men cut me off. One of them has magic and shoots off a couple of jolts of magical energy.

I duck the blasts of orange magic and a tree explodes bark behind me. Rolling to the side, I find cover behind a tree. There's nowhere to go.

Lukas is busy casting and seems to be negating the spells of my attacker. I peer around the tree and search for my father. "Where fuck is he?"

In the split-second, I glance away, the tallest of the attackers grabs something out of his belt. The metallic edge glints gold in the light of the fire.

With sickening speed, the man unleashes the dagger into the air. I follow the trajectory and curse when I see Brant standing directly in its path. Our bear is grappling with an attacker and doesn't see the danger.

"Brant!"

He turns but doesn't have time to avoid the hit. All he can do is throw up his arm and block.

In a blur of movement so fast my eyes barely register it, Yarko throws up his hand and the air swallows the dagger. The kid swings his hand back toward the influx of Black Knight minions and the blade reappears and impales one of their own.

I'm staring in wonder when Jaxx cages me into his arms and spins us out of the path of another approaching blade.

Kotah moves in fast, plucks the dagger out of the air, and without hesitation sends it end-over-end back to its owner.

The blade sinks true. The attacker's hands grasp at the hilt of the weapon lodged in his throat as he crumples. Blood fountains through his clenched fingers, pooling like oil and seeping into the soil of the forest floor.

Three others stepped over him and advance.

Damn, how many men does he have? The forest is seething with men in black gear and I curse. We're so fucking outnumbered it's pathetic.

I scan the surroundings, assessing where my mates are when a burst of magic rushes through the clearing. One minute we're getting overrun by the enemy, and the next, they're gone and the forest falls eerily quiet.

"What happened?" I snap. "Where are they?"

"Gone," Lukas says. He's standing with his hands on his hips scowling at the empty space where my father had been tethered for the past hour.

"Fuuuuck!" I shout. "How the fuck did this happen? Where's Rowan? And where's the kid?"

Lukas shakes his head. "It shouldn't have happened. That spell was a lock. None of his men we've come up against had the juice needed to break it."

"The greater fae tree freak does," Brant snaps.

Lukas frowns. "Why would Rowan set Sabastian free when he helped us capture him?"

The air snaps with the arrival of a traveler. Yarko appears and holds out his hand. "Okay, hurry. We followed them and know where they went."

No one grabs on.

"What? Don't you want to get Sabastian back?"

Brant moves to grab the kid's hand and I stop the contact. "No, don't. This stinks of a double-cross. I'd rather let my father walk now and be sure of our next move. I wondered why he was so calm. This is exactly the kind of mind-fuck he'd pull. The whole enemy of my enemy is my friend bullshit could be a ploy."

Brant chuckles. "Awesome. So, now we're back to

thinking the Forest Lord is a bad guy?"

"No, he's not," Yarko snaps. "You don't want to come, fine. I'm not leaving him on his own."

The kid flashes out and we're still standing there wondering what the hell happened when Rowan flashes back. He lifts my father's severed head by the hair and scowls. "You gave me your word and I am a man of honor. Your father escaped and I tracked him. Come or don't but fifty narys just witnessed me slice his head off, so there will be repercussions."

"Fuck." I stare at the gruesome head dripping onto the soil below. My father is dead? There's so much I need to reconcile about that but there's no time. "Amir and Andy, secure the portal rift. Doc and Keyla, hold the fort. Lukas, you're with us."

Calli grips Rowan's arm and Jaxx's cat lets off a ferocious growl. "Calli should stay here with Doc and Keyla. Establishing a portal gate is her destiny. Seriously, Hawk. Leave her here. She's been shot twice today already. How much are you willing to risk for your father's bullshit?"

I hate the fear in his eyes and know it's all about the baby. I'm worried too but Calli is a strong, independent woman and has the greatest chance of survival out of all of us.

Calli frowns. "I'm not sure who pissed in your cat box, puss, but even if Sabastian laid a trap, we can handle it together like always. You don't get to leave me behind."

I nod to Rowan. "Six of us, locked and loaded."

Jaxx

Before I can argue, the six of us, plus Rowan, and Sabastian's head materialize beside Yarko and Sabastian's body. They're tucked behind an outdoor screen of a smoking corral attached to the side of a twenty-story, steel and glass office building. I assess the body more out of habit being a paramedic than because I believe he might still have a pulse. But, after seeing Hawk put three bullets into his chest earlier and him getting back up, it can't hurt to be thorough.

"And?" Hawk asks as if he is thinking the same thing.

"Definitely dead. Your theory was correct."

"Holy shit, Hawk," Brant says. "Look where we are."

The two of us straighten and I look down the block at… "Wait. Isn't that the FCO building?"

As an FCO First Responder, I never came to the Manhattan head office, but as Hawk's mate, we were attacked here a week or two ago by Sabastian's men.

Hawk studies the cityscape and freezes in place.

It sinks in then. His father set up shop across the road from his building to actively destroy him. How long was he here? How long had he planned this? Hunter worked here for three years. That's messed up.

I know Hawk is losing his shit because our avian has a tell. First, he clenches his jaw tight enough you'd swear he's going to snap off his back molars, and then a vein starts throbbing beside his temple.

Other people probably don't notice, but once Calli pointed it out to me, it's hard not to see.

Pulling out his phone, he calls up a contact and hits send. "Jayne, I need a full breach team and two field teams down the road at 9525. Yes, you heard me… Not now… Jayne, just send the fucking teams. A Forest Lord decapitated my father in front of the building. They can't miss it. And have Mallory Daniford from the security desk come too. I need his skills."

He hangs up and tucks his phone back into his pocket. "Okay, next dilemma. Do we know where the dervishes are being held?"

"No, but I feel them inside," Rowan says.

"Have we got any idea what kind of security protocols they have for gaining access to the building?"

Rowan lifts Sabastian's head. "Retinal scanning and a key card."

"Your father was a paranoid freak," Yarko says.

Hawk nods. "If you stab enough people in the back, you get that way. Brant, search for his card."

After a moment of going through the man's pockets, our bear comes up with a card wallet and tosses it to Hawk. "So, are we ready to rumble?"

Lukas pulls a small silver case out of his flack vest. He pries open the lid and turns it until the clear earbuds nestled in black foam are facing us. "Everyone, grab one and tap the little button before you put it in your ear. It's easier that way if you're not accustomed to using them."

We do as we're told.

Hawk finishes going through his father's cards and holds up two possible winners. "I'm good. Are you guys set?"

Not even close. I look at Calli and unlike other times

when we've been marching into battle and all I saw was her almost indestructible strength, now all I see is the vulnerability of what violence against her could cost us.

Today she got shot in the shoulder and the knee. What if she got shot in the abdomen? "Stay close and stay safe, kitten."

Calli squeezes my hand. "S'all good, puss."

"Ready," Brant says, anticipation lacing his smile.

"I will come too," Rowan says. "Exposure is no longer an issue—which I am sorry about—but I refused to let him escape. Now that your team is coming to negate exposure, I wish to go inside and join the fight."

"Are the people inside all his or does he have a floor?"

"All his," Yarko says.

"How can you know that for sure?"

The kid shrugs. "I read the directory in the foyer."

Brant stretches his neck and cracks his knuckles. "Pitter-patter let's bring down this house of cards."

Hawk checks the skyline and looks up the side of the building. "Rowan, portal to the roof with Kotah, and Lukas. The three of you sweep each floor and work your way down. Calli, Brant, and I will take my father's head and go in from the ground. We'll work our way up and meet you in the middle. Yarko, you stay here and when my teams arrive, fill them in and have them secure anyone trying to leave the building."

The kid frowns. "No. I want to fight. I was more affected by what they did than all of you."

"Which is why you sit this out, sorry. I need you here to direct our backup and handle the scene. We've got fae exposure and that takes priority."

The kid's not happy about the answer but seems to accept that it's a done deal.

Kotah kisses Calli and then he, Lukas, and Rowan flash out. Brant and I flank Calli. I know Hawk's choice of putting the two most violently protective mates at her side isn't a coincidence. There is thought behind everything he does.

CHAPTER FIFTEEN

Hawk

The four of us cross the vast concrete pad in front of the building and Calli and Brant walk beside me, shielding the fact that we're carrying a severed head. My stride falters at the site of where Rowan caught up with him. There's a massive pool of blood darkening the concrete and it's splattered up the side of the building. It's good they moved the body into the smoking area because this looks like a scene from a slasher flick.

My father is dead.

The reality of that hasn't set in yet.

I should be horrified or rocked to some degree. I think I am… but I'm numb. Am I glad to be rid of him or sad because now I'll never prove to him how wrong he was about me?

"Hey there. Are you okay?"

I meet the sympathetic gaze of Calli and swallow. "No. I don't think I am. Stupid, eh?"

"Not stupid at all, hotness," Jaxx says, squeezing my shoulder. "Unfortunately, you need to store your conflict away until this is over. We need focus so no one gets hurt."

The look he shoots me makes it clear who the 'no one' he's worried about getting hurt is.

"Baggage about your father is yet another issue to deal with when we have our little private time chat," Calli says. "Things are piling up."

Brant pulls the handle on the glass door and we step inside. I hand Jaxx the head and Brant pulls out the key cards. "This is easy enough. The logo matches." He swipes the card and then Jaxx positions things so the retinal scanner reads my father's eye.

The inner door latch clicks and we're in.

"Jaxx, hold the door. Brant, grab that chair and prop the entrance open so our backup can get in."

Brant makes quick work of that and then we fan out and cross the polished floor of the entrance.

"I'm surprised there isn't anyone working the front door," Calli says."

"There will be guards watching monitors somewhere close by. Keep your eyes open. We want one of them to talk to."

"Hey, stop! What are you doing here?" The male voice echoes in the marble and glass lobby and we turn to find two men rushing at us. "Who gave you authorization to be here?"

Brant swaggers up to them and then when he gets close, he bursts into flying fists. In a split-second, one's unconscious and the other is in a sleeper hold.

"Damn, our offensive moves have leveled up," I say.

Calli grins. "Did anyone else find that super sexy?"

Jaxx raises a hand.

I adjust the partial filling out my fly. "Yeah, insta-horny over here but yeah-no, not the time."

Brant chuckles and waggles his brow. "Who says being sexually objectified is a bad thing? Okay, boss, now what?"

I pull out my phone and make a call. "All clear, Mallory. Please step inside the entrance."

A moment later my night guard from headquarters steps through the front door with four FCO Enforcers. "Sir Barron, always a pleasure. How may I help you, sir?"

I meet the male with an extended palm. "Thank you for coming, Mallory. I'm hoping you can save us time and energy. The Black Knight is working out of this location and has taken innocents hostage. I wonder if you can find out where they're being held and with what security precautions?"

"Of course, sir. I'd be happy to help."

I step back as the man's tail extends and uncoils, encircling the guard several times around.

"Go ahead and ask your questions, sir. He should be willing to speak freely to you."

I repeat my questions and although the guard doesn't seem to want to comply with my request for information, as a member of the hulderfolk, Mallory's powers for drawing the truth out of people is impossible to fight.

"Fourth floor. Retinal scan and key card to open the door of the elevator and a keypad to access the detainment floor."

"And what's the punch code for the keypad?"

"I don't know. Only Mr. Whitehouse and his son know."

Awesome. Hunter, my half-brother douche, is the only person alive who knows the code. "That's fine. Lukas can bypass it, I'm sure."

I nod to the men who came in with Mallory. "Secure these two and anyone who tries to leave. No one gets out of here until we have the hostages freed and go through this building top to bottom. One team is on sweep, the other will detain. Any questions?"

"No sir," the team leader says.

When they're set on their tasks, I turn back and rest my hand on Mallory's shoulder so he can read my sincerity. "Thank you, my friend. Much appreciated. If you don't mind staying, I'd like to talk to you about another matter when we're finished."

Mallory beams, as always, with any amount of genuine praise. "Yes, sir. Happy to be of service, sir. Nice to see you again, Mr. Robbins."

Brant pats Mallory on the shoulder as he passes. "Nice to see you too, buddy. Thanks for the shortcut."

Brant, Jaxx, Calli, and I jog toward the elevator and I activate my earpiece. "Hostages are being held on the fourth floor. We're headed there now. Clear each floor as you come down. You've got friendlies coming up to relieve you."

In the elevator, I stick the keycard into the slot and point to the retinal scanner. Jaxx does his part with my father's noggin and the elevator gets moving.

"What species is Mallory?" Calli asks.

"Hulderfolk. They're like a walking lie detector race. They can't lie and they can force truths from others. Perfect for security. Not to mention he's a helluva solid male."

The elevator doors open on the fourth floor and we're sucked into a storm of fighting soldiers. Rowan and a dozen men are clashing hard, my father's men hell-bent on keeping us out of the detainment area.

"Shit. How'd he get here before us?"

Sizing up our surroundings, Jaxx mutters a low oath and shifts to jaguar. Brant drops to all fours and his bear joins the party. The quarters are too close for guns, so I draw my knife from my thigh-sheath and engage in the melee.

Calli strips quickly and dives in beside me. She heats up to her female on fire form and faces off like the fiery fury she is. Within seconds she's sending a scalding swath of flames through security men and they're doing their best to stay out of her way.

We don't feel her molten heat the way others do, but by their hasty retreats, I imagine she's a living wall of scalding heat. I duck the swipe of a blade coming in from the side, narrowly escaping decapitation by a sickening few inches.

How's that for life's ironies—my father and I both losing our heads on the same night after not seeing one another for almost twenty years?

Crazy.

The guy who came at me is the size of a giant redwood. He is a roid-droid, unnatural mass of muscle and brawn—and that's his most attractive quality. "Has anyone ever told you that your face looks like a scrotum?"

On a roar, he thrusts forward, swinging that machete blade at me again. A solid elbow coming down on his wrist knocks the weapon out of the fight and then it's fists against fists.

He's big but clunky. I bend backward when his right hook whistles past my face. He comes at me again.

The *whoosh* of flames hiss in my ear as a fireball zings past me and takes the guy to the floor in a fiery blaze.

"Hey, I had him."

Calli

I chuckle at Hawk's indignation that I fireballed his opponent. "I know, surly. I just think fireballs are badass and ran out of guys to throw them at."

Adrenaline burns through my veins, and my next flaming projectile comes off like a crack of lightning. It barrels across the room, exploding against the back of some unsuspecting brute. Too soon, we've taken control of the fight and the bad guys are either dead or giving up.

Quitters.

"Where are Lukas and Kotah?" Hawk snaps the moment the fighting falls silent.

Rowan straightens the horn around his neck and rises to his full height. "I left them when you said the prisoners are on four. This is the reason I'm here. To rescue my family."

The shriek of a captive inside the detainment area

has us focusing on how to get through to the other side.

"Yeah, to rescue *our* families. I get that you're not much of a team player, but we've got missing people too."

Rowan doesn't seem to care.

"Can you transport us inside there?" I ask.

He shakes his massive elk rack, and dagger-sharp horns swing in the air. "See those globes in the corners in there? Those are magic suppressors. Nothing magical will work in there."

"Lukas, I need you on four," Hawk says.

"Almost there. Our ride ditched us."

"Yeah, we know. He's here."

Brant drags a few men out of the doorway and lines them up against the wall. When he straightens, he catches my glance and flashes me a sexy smile. The gleam on his face darkens at the same time the hair on my neck stands on end.

I spin and call my fire as the hiss of steel cuts through the air. In a slow-motion moment like on TV, I see the dagger fly straight at my stomach. End over end, it glints in the stark white light of the fluorescents.

Just before it impales me, my majestic jungle cat leaps through the air and takes me to the ground. Stunned, I struggle under the crush of the weight of Jaxx's cat.

Brant's bear lets off an enraged roar and then there's a snap so loud I don't want to look at what he did to whoever threw that knife.

"*Jaxx!*" Hawk is there in an instant, rolling our jaguar off me and checking the wound. "The blade is lodged in his side, between his ribs. It could've punctured a lung or nicked any number of vital organs including his heart. Calli, you need to do your thing."

I raise a shaky hand to his round, velvety cheek.

Crying won't be a problem. Seeing him like this breaks my heart. We've come full circle. In those first hours when I didn't understand this world and thought I was their prisoner, I hurt him. It was a desperate attempt for survival. I didn't realize how badly he was hurt, but it still haunts me how close we came to losing him.

I can't imagine losing any of them. I can't. Kotah, Brant, Hawk, and Jaxx are my life. "Jaxx, I've got you."

Lukas and Kotah rush through the door beside the elevator and join the chaos. Hawk rises to tackle the door lock while I work myself to tears for Jaxx.

"What happened?" Kotah kneels beside me.

I looked from the emotion in our wolf's eyes to our fallen mate and embrace the sting of oncoming tears. "One of the men threw a knife. He shouldn't have jumped in the way. Now he's suffering. I hate it when you boys suffer."

As the tears start to flow, I curl my body around my jungle cat. "You should've let the blade hit my stomach. It would've hurt, but I heal faster."

"No, he shouldn't," Kotah says, stroking a gentle caress over Jaxx's coat. "He was right to protect you from harm. It's our job as your guardians, your mates, and the fathers of our baby. That's what we wanted to tell you in private. Five become one. You're pregnant. If that knife went through your belly…."

I swipe the tears blurring my vision and wipe the

moisture on his wound. "What? Pregnant?"

He nods. "That's why you've been so tired and hungry."

"How can you possibly know that before me?" Tears roll down my cheek and drip off my chin and onto Jaxx's wound.

"It's in your scent, *Chigua*. I smelled it this afternoon in the forest."

"When you goobed me?"

He smiles. "It's faint but unmistakable."

A baby? I gather more moisture off my cheeks and point to the hilt of the knife still embedded in Jaxx's side. "I can't deal with this right now. Let me focus on healing Jaxx."

With our gazes locked, Kotah pulls the knife. Jaxx lets off a hideous sound and my gut twists. I press my damp fingers over the wound and my heart breaks a little more.

Tears fall in a torrent and I set them free.

Crying isn't even an effort this time.

Hawk and Lukas break the lock down and move to rescue the innocent people. When Lukas pushes the door open, he's nearly flattened by Rowan as the Forest Lord races ahead.

The heavy *thunk, thunk, thunk* as the tree man runs down the corridor shakes the floor beneath my knees. Hawk helps Lukas to his feet and then the two of them head in to search the prison cells.

"Go help them, sweet prince. I've got Jaxx." I bend over Jaxx and give him another dousing in magical healing.

Kotah

I race into the detainment area of the fourth floor in the wake of Rowan, Lukas, and Hawk. The building is set up with one main corridor running the length of the floor and off-shoot corridors branching left and right every fifty feet or so.

Hawk waves me down the first corridor on the left and I change course. I'm eager to find Mother and Raven if they're here, but if not, get back to Jaxx and Calli. Logic tells me Jaxx will be fine and Brant will never let anything happen to them but leaving them feels wrong on all fronts.

Still, it *is* my mother we're searching for.

Despite our contentious relationship, I never wanted anything like this to happen to her. Maybe in a convoluted way, fate stepped in to teach me a hard truth because her abduction has made me realize I still care.

"Kotah," Hawk says, up ahead. "We have your mother. She looks unharmed."

I jog up the hall and peer past where Lukas is working on the door's locking mechanisms. Leaning in, I wave and offer my mother what I hope is a comforting smile. "I'd say she looks more pissed than unharmed."

Hawk chuckles, his back to her cell. "She is a delight to deal with at the best of times."

"And this won't be one of those."

"No. I don't expect it will."

Absently, I wander across the hall and look inside the opposite containment room. There's an old man with birchbark skin and mossy hair sleeping on a single bed.

Glancing down the hallway, I count the glass windows and start doing the math. "Are there fae prisoners in all of them?"

Hawk runs a rough hand over his face and frowns. "No idea. A lot of them, anyway. What the fuck were my father and Hunter up to?"

"I have no idea, but I think it goes deeper than screwing you over and keeping the two realms from uniting."

I wander up the hall a little and calculate the scope of what we're dealing with. There are three doors on each side of the hall, so six prison cubicles on this branch and another six on the right, and another three branches. I do some quick math and frown. "If all the cubicles are prisons of the same size, there are forty-eight cells on this floor."

"Fuck me," Hawk pulls out his cell and makes another call. "Me again. I need you down here to assess the impact of what we're dealing with. This is much bigger than we thought. Fourth floor. Bring medical response, a couple of event recovery people, and a few extra bodies to document and collect names and personal accounts of what happened."

He hangs up and I see the weight of this pressing down on him. I move in tight and press my hand on the side of his throat, easing his turmoil. "This isn't your fault. None of this is your doing. Leave the blame squarely where it belongs—on your father's head."

"Literally or figuratively because it just so happens, I'm now in possession of his head."

I don't know whether to chuckle or hug him. Opting for the latter, I wrap my arms around his ribs and nuzzle against his throat. "I'm sorry you're so twisted up about this mess. I wish we were still on the couch shutting out the world."

He eases back and cups my jaw, teasing the seam of my lips with his tongue. "So, do I, Wolf. Let's do that again, first chance we get."

"It's a date."

"We're ready here," Lukas says.

We break it up and head back to the cubicle where my mother's been held prisoner.

Lukas gets the door open and my mother shrugs on her wrap. "Thank you, gentlemen. I'm pleased to see you got around to finding me. I admit I wondered how much of a priority the past Prima would be."

I take a deep breath and step into the line of fire. "Of course, you're a priority, Mother. You are a beloved figure of the realm. And you have only been the Past Prima for one day, so you're hardly obsolete and forgotten."

I escort her out of the prison cubicle and give her my elbow as we head down the hallway.

"Where is Raven? Have you found her?"

"Not yet, Prima," Hawk says. "There are dozens of cells to search and unlock. Your safety was our primary concern. If she's here, we'll find her."

Mother looks at me and frowns. "I'd like a seat so I can wait while you search. Raven is important to me and I won't enjoy my freedom while her fate is yet unknown."

"Alright, that's fine."

Lukas brings the chair out of Mother's cubicle and

we get her set up in the hallway. I think about bringing her up to the front near Calli and the elevators, but with the murder and mayhem splattered around, and Calli raw about the baby, I decide to keep her back here as long as possible.

"It is a disappointment a madman disrupted your coronation, Nakotah. What must people think? And without Raven to handle the optics, it's probably public knowledge by now."

I clasp my hands behind my back. "There was a mass shooting and assassination attempt at the royal coronation. There's no need to spin the attack to my advantage, Mother. It's what happened and everyone who was there knows it had nothing to do with our family and everything to do with the Black Knight. If people choose to twist that, let them."

Mother chuckles. "Oh, how naïve you are, my son. Perhaps one day soon you'll wake up and realize you should've listened to your mother more often."

"Perhaps." *I doubt it.*

Jaxx

Lying in a pool of death and blood, my cat is content in the knowledge that the battle is over, and my mate and child are unharmed. I purr as Calli's touch slides over the silk of my coat and the last of my pain ebbs into a faded memory.

I should shift back so we can join the others. I just don't want to. Is it so wrong to need two minutes of quiet affection before facing the next challenge?

"I love you, puss," Calli says, her face nuzzled close

to my ear. "I love you hard."

Brant rubs a hand over my hip and pats my ass. "Welcome back, my man. Good job on the block. FYI, Kotah spilled the beans."

Okay, damn, now I have to shift back. I shift back and flash on my clothes, rolling from my side to sit up. "How freaked are you? Scale of one to ten?"

"A thousand," Calli says, her eyes still red-rimmed from crying. "Is it so wrong that I wanted more time with you four before our relationship changed? Does that make me selfish? Am I already a horrible mother?"

I scootch back a bit to lean against the wall and pull her into my lap. "No. I understand completely why you want to protect our adult time. It's life-altering and it should be cherished. What we have is more than the drunken game nights and the down and dirty naked gymnastics. There are times when the five of us share things that change the course of our future. We are everything."

"Exactly. And that's enough for me."

I press my lips against her temple and breathe her in. Closing my eyes, I try to detect the subtle change in her scent that Kotah smells. I think I do. There's something. There's just no way I could be as sure as he is that it's a baby.

"Do you remember that first day when I explained things to you in the garden?"

Her face pales and I know where her mind went.

"Not that. Before that, when we were still sittin' in the gazebo, I told you there's no rush or need for you to say anythin'. I'm here for you, whatever you need."

She swallows. "I remember."

"I also told you this is forever. You don't have to take on the world alone ever again. We're a team."

"I understand all that, Jaxx, and I have no doubts about the five of us, but I don't even know what to do with the idea that I'm growing a person who's going to need me to have my shit together. I don't have my shit together."

I chuckle and she sends me a scathing scowl.

"Okay, how about this? How about we dedicate ourselves to as much adult fun as we can pack in until the baby thing takes priority. We still have four or five months before it'll even be more than a bump on your belly. By then, I promise you, we'll have our shit together. The rift is open, we'll work on the bridge and the gate next."

"Look how far you came in three months," Brant says, squatting down beside us. He brushes the back of his fingers against her cheek and smiles. "With twice as much time, you'll be a fucking Rockstar."

"I think you both have a skewed idea of who I am and what I'm capable of."

Brant chuckles and his deep timbre rolls through the air around us. "One thing the four of us are very clear on is who you are and what you're capable of, beautiful. If Jaxx says we can do this, I believe him. He's the one who knows, after all. Let's trust him."

Calli looks at me like she wants to argue but at least she's not freaking out anymore. "Tell me that wildling bodies don't get all stretched and saggy after a baby. Tell me I'll still be me this time next year."

I smile. Next year seems like an age to wait, but with a baby on the way, I'm sure time will fly. "This time next year, you'll be a new and improved version of the female you are right now. And the bonus… we'll have our baby."

I give her one last, long hug and then get us both to our feet. "Now, let's go find our mates and see how close we are to getting out of here and back to the clearing to secure the portal rift."

"I, for one, am looking forward to pitching a tent and then pitching a tent," Brant says, pointing to the front of his pants. "See what I did there?"

We both chuckle and I pat Brant's shoulder as we make our way into the detainment area. "Yeah, Bear. I saw what you did. Now let's see what we're dealin' with so we can get gone. I'm done with today."

CHAPTER SIXTEEN

Kotah

It amazes me how much simply sitting on a log, staring into a fire, next to my mate means to me. Do I wish we were naked and alone? Absolutely. Despite the fact that Hawk's construction crew arrived while we were in Manhattan raiding the Black Knight headquarters last night, it'll take time before the bridge is established and the gate is secured.

Once that happens, all bets are off.

This quint needs some downtime.

It seems ungrateful to ask for more than what the universe has given us. Calli is well, she opened the rift to establish the portal gate, and best of all—she's having our baby.

"I'm glad your mom's safe," Calli says, leaning my way to rub shoulders.

I kiss her temple and breathe her in. "I am, as well, but honestly, it pales next to how blessed I feel knowing the five of us are together and whole, and our task is almost complete. As much as I've loved our adventures, I'm ready for a month of Jaxx's games and snuggling in to watch movies."

I must've said something right because she exhales a long sigh and smiles. "That sounds like heaven."

It does. "Yesterday was tough. When the portal gate blew you back and we couldn't get to you before those men started shooting. The helplessness of it was life-shattering. And then, to know someone almost impaled you only hours later… you don't even know how that would have destroyed us."

"I love you too, sweet prince, soul-deep, and forever."

I catch Mother watching us, but don't acknowledge her. She's standing at the food table with my sister and Raven. She's still wearing her extravagant gown from the coronation and looks as uncomfortable in the forest as anyone could.

She's a wildling who doesn't embrace her wolf.

I can't even imagine.

My heart makes a promise to our baby right then. We will never forget or deny the duality of our species. We are wildlings and as such, half of us belongs to nature. I may be forced to *work* in a palace, but I'll never be forced to *live* in one or raise our child in one.

I'm the Fae Prime, after all.

I'm the man.

"Good morning, mates," Brant says, settling on the ground beside us. He has a heaping plate of leftovers from last night and a characteristic grin on his face. "Doesn't get much better, does it? Mates, food, forest, friends, enemy neutralized and destiny realized."

And a baby on the way. Brant's smart not to mention that one. Calli might not be actively freaking out, but she's definitely not reconciled to the idea of being a mother.

Yet.

Jaxx's pep talk bought us some time. In the months to come, we'll prove to her it'll be alright. There's nothing the four of us want more than to make her and our baby happy.

Mother casts me a disapproving scowl.

She's never been interested in what makes me happy. How did she miss out on this feeling of love and dedication so completely?

"Your mother's in fine form this morning," Brant says, chuckling as he chews. "She's bending your sister's ear about how she's suffered. Imagine, the indignity of being captured and contained for one whole day."

I chuckle inwardly. "One day. She was displaced and alone for one day and thinks the sky is falling. She truly has no idea what my life has been like."

Calli hugs me and sets her chin on my shoulder. "Your old life. And like Hawk says, everything that came before brought us here as the people we are. That which doesn't kill us makes us stronger."

"That's right, beautiful," Brant says, finishing with his plate. "If we can tone down the parts where you get shot and stabbed going forward, we'd all appreciate it."

Calli reaches forward and runs her fingers into the waves of Brant's dark brown hair. "I don't remember much after getting shot. I didn't suffer much because, by the time I woke up, my healing ability had taken hold."

"Then thank the Powers you blacked out."

She laughs and rolls her eyes. "Blacked out, naked in front of everyone. *Again.* Yeah, thank the Powers that be. At least tell me I did it with flare."

I cast a sideways glance and smile. "It was very elegant, *Chigua.* You didn't even faceplant."

Calli meets my gaze and scowls. "For reals or are you saying I *did* faceplant and you're teasing me?"

Brant chuckles and she rolls her eyes. "Perfect. But not too many people saw it, right?"

"Just us, and Sabastian's men," I point to the depths of the forest and smile. "And perhaps a few dozen fae creatures."

Calli follows my finger and sits straighter. "One day, I'd like to meet new people and not be naked."

I brush a piece of hair from her face. "Don't give it a second thought. The fae community is in awe of what you've done here. As are we all."

"Yeah," Brant says, "seeing you naked doesn't register for them in the grand scheme of things like it does for us." *But the more important question is when we'll get to see you naked next and not have to rush. I was making shadow puppets by the light of the fire last night with the tent I'm pitching.*

Calli snorts and covers the outburst with a cough. "Hawk is working on that."

He needs to work faster or I'll whisk you back into the trees to go au naturel *on you again. You boys in?*

Jaxx saunters over from the treeline with a predatory swagger in those powerful hips of his. He waggles his brow in all his blond, Texas cowboy beauty and smiles. "Hells yeah, I'm in."

"In for what?" Keyla asks, her attention drawn from the other side of the fire. "Or don't I want to know?"

Brant chuckles. "Likely not, little sista."

Calli gestures a lazy finger to the eyes glowing in the trees. "So, when you said dozens of fae creatures, what did you mean?"

Keyla looks around and nods. "I sensed them in the forest while we were running last night. What are they, sprites?"

I shake my head. "Pixies and fire dervishes. The ones from last night, with the citrine eyes, are fire dervishes. They are excited by the flames and are likely drawn to Calli herself, but probably won't come out. The pixies, though, are getting more curious and have made contact. See, Hawk's speaking to one over by the seam of the rift. By the look of her and the way the others are hovering, I'd wager a bet that's their queen."

Calli shifts her attention and I hear her intake of breath.

I remember the first time I ever saw pixies. I thought them so strange… dozens of little flying creatures with pointy teeth and equally pointy ears. They're no bigger than a raven but their wings are less feathery and more stretched leather like a bat's.

We sit quietly for a few beats and then Calli tilts her head back and stares into the canopy of the trees above us. "I think our guests have decided to join us."

"Actually," a midnight blue pixie says, "this is our land, child. It's *you* who would be the guests."

Hawk nods to the woman who spoke and holds his hand out to help Calli off the log. "Astute as always,

Queen."

Calli

I accept Hawk's hand and stand for the arrival of the blue lady with all the teeth. She flutters and flaps in the jerky, erratic way that a bat does and settles close by on a sturdy, low-hanging branch. It doesn't matter that the Pixie Queen is no bigger than my forearm, she's a queen—and a freaky looking one at that. "Your Majesty, it's nice to meet you."

"Thank you, Phoenix," the lady says, dropping her pointy chin. "It is nice to meet you as well. It seems you fulfilled your destiny yesterday. Congratulations."

Yesterday? Cray-cray.

It feels like days ago.

Hawk rests a protective arm across my back and squeezes my shoulder. "Calliope Tannis, this is DenysTa, Queen of the Pixies. It seems, she and her community inhabit the land on this side of the river."

"And were you part of the plan to disguise the former site of the portal gate? Or was that solely Rowan?"

The Pixie Queen's smile exposes several rows of jagged teeth. "I am a queen. Everything that happens on my land is mine to claim."

That doesn't answer my question, but I don't pursue it.

"Well, I hope you'll excuse us all tromping around and waging war in the forest. It couldn't be helped and was very important."

"Important to say the least," she agrees, sweeping a

hand toward the energy flux glittering in the air like oil on water. The iridescence of the magic is being reflected by the morning light and is quite pretty. "What you did here yesterday is a miraculous feat."

Hawk kisses my temple and winks. "She's a wonder."

I shake that off but get a little lost in the warmth of his smile. "You, Sir Barron, were the one to figure out where we needed to be."

He arches an ebony brow and sends me a cocky look. "And you figured out what you needed to do."

Brant chuckles. "Okay, you two enough with the counter-flattery-flirtery—you both rock our socks. Don't they?"

Kotah and Jaxx both laugh and agree.

The pixie queen flaps her wings and catches our attention again. "The pixies are, of course, thrilled the gate is underway and understand arrangements and accommodations must be made while it's being established. However, with the portal gate falling on my private property, there is much to discuss in the way of compensation, levies, and passage fees."

I catch the surprise on the faces of my mates and agree.

She wants compensation to use land stolen from the fae in the first place? Brant asks privately.

Jaxx chuckles. *Yeah-no, I can't see that happening.*

With pixies, nothing is ever as it seems, Hawk says. *This is where my fun begins. Life is one big negotiation. Kotah this will be your first lesson in Prime politics. Care to play?*

Kotah frowns. *I'm not ready for something as big as this. DenysTa scares me... always has.*

Hawk's chin dips in a subtle nod. *That just proves how intelligent you are, Wolf. Don't worry, we'll navigate this together. I won't let her take advantage of you.*

Calli

I'm not sure why I expect the Queen of Pixies to have a palace like the one Kotah's family has, but yeah, okay, they are the size of birds, so that doesn't make sense. However you look at it, my hope of curling up on a couch for twenty minutes and having a nap while the guys hammer out terms is dashed. Back to the tent, it is.

"Calli, one sec," Lukas says, calling me over to where he and Hawk's men are unpacking crates. He hands me a box and points at the picture on the front. "I believe this was meant for you."

I grin from ear to ear and hold it up for Jaxx to see. "A foam mattress. Just what I wanted."

Jaxx chuckles. "That's our avian. Always anticipating our needs. Come on, let's take it to the tent and get it set up."

"Forget the tent," Doc says jogging over with a hammer in his hand. "It's not much, but we have the first two tiny houses framed and sided. You're welcome to claim one and get off the forest floor."

Brant comes loping out of the trees, his hands cupped and overflowing with berries. "Did I hear you say we have walls and a door?"

"And a comfy foam topper," I add, showing him my

box.

"Booyah!" Brant says. "Lead the way, my brother. Let's check out the new digs."

Jaxx chuckles. "And when you say check out…"

Doc rolls his eyes and turns back the way he came. "We all know what he means. Just keep in mind that we've got workers busily building temporary lodgings right next door. We don't want to hear your throaty throes of orgasm."

Brant snorts. "Then hammer and saw as loud as you can and you won't hear us. Otherwise… orgasms baby."

"Keyla and I thought Calli might want to rest," he says. "You know… because she was so tired yesterday and that was before the day went to shit."

"And before you all found out I'm preggers," I add.

He grins. "I wasn't sure if you knew yet. Keyla smelled it in your scent yesterday, but she said it's very faint. I can't smell it at all."

Brant grins. "The wolves for the olfactory win. Kotah smelled it too."

Doc smacks Brant on the shoulder and points to a freshly hewn wooden cube at the edge of the treeline. "Then let me congratulate you all on your cub. It's amazing news. This is you. Enjoy. And I promise we'll hammer loudly."

I roll my eyes, my cheeks flaring hot. "So, much for taking a nap. Now they're going to intentionally make noise.

Jaxx chuckles as we duck inside our lodgings. "We'll make do, kitten. And maybe we can exhaust you enough that you'll sleep through the noise."

"Worth a try," Brant says, closing the door behind us.

I scan the interior and smile. It's a simple square box with a plank floor, four walls, and a roof that slopes toward a bed platform against the back wall. We've got enough space at the front for a kitchenette counter to be put in and a café table with two chairs and that's it.

"It's cute," I say. "It's clean and private and that raised platform is the perfect place to spread out my foam topper."

"And smells like freshly cut pine," Jaxx says.

"And we have a snack," Brant says, holding out his berry-filled palms. "Unpack your mattress and then I'll use the box as a tray."

I undo the box and hand it off to Brant.

Jaxx and I unfold the topper, and the moment it's free of its cellophane confinement, it starts to self-inflate. I giggle. "Look how eager it is to become our bed."

"Smart foam," Jaxx says, rucking my shirt over my head.

"We're all set," Brant says, going for his button fly.

Cool air hits my skin and my nipples tighten. "How long do you think it'll take Kotah and Hawk to iron out things with the queen?"

Jaxx chuckles, skimming his fingers down my hips and shoving my pants to the new floor. "I'm sure as soon as they feel us getting' our grove on through the mate bond, they'll wrap up as quick as a hiccup."

Once Brant and I are naked, the two of us make quick work of relieving Jaxx from his clothes. The fact that our jaguar goes commando always calls a mad heat from within me.

I yank on the two sides of his shirt open and the snaps give way in one violent surrender. "Look at all that delicious, golden skin."

Jaxx's cat growls and the low, predatory sound makes my ache increase. "You hungry today, kitten?"

"I am. I don't know if it's the relief of having the portal gate under control or my hormones or the fresh air but I need a sixty-nine in the worst way."

Brant barks a laugh. "I volunteer as tribute."

The three of us crawl onto the platform and after sleeping on the forest floor with a camp mat last night, this foam mattress is cushiony bliss.

"How sturdy do you think this platform is?" Brant says, his chest bouncing with amusement as he rolls me on my back. He crawls over me, suckling on my nipples, his hair sweeping the bare skin of my chest. "It would be a shame to bust it the same day they made it."

"Not to mention embarrassing," I add, arching off the mattress to meet his kiss.

Jaxx chuckles, crawling to the top of the bed and placing my hand on his hard cock. Sitting back on his knees, his eyes roll shut as I stroke his length. "Oh, yeah. Now I think we should put it to the test. You know… quality assurance."

Brant raises his head from my breast and smiles when he sees Jaxx's crown peek out of my hold when I slide my stroke down his shaft. "You've sprung a leak there, mate. Need some help with that?"

"If you're offerin', I'll never say no."

I watch in rapture as Brant shifts to the side and

sucks Jaxx's cock in right to where my hand is propping him up.

"So hot," I breathe, reaching between Brant's legs until I have a mate erection in each hand. "Suck him off, Brant. Pull him deep into your mouth while I feel how it turns you on."

In answer to my request, his cock pulses in my grip, and his hips pump into my hold.

"Yeah, like that. More of that."

Brant's head starts to bob over Jaxx's lap, and I scissor my thighs as a rush of cream moistens my pussy. Squeezing my fingers tighter around Brant's cock, I slide the velvet skin over the solid shaft.

"How good is that, Jaxx?"

Our jaguar swallows and grunts, gripping Brant's hair and flexing his hips. "So good…"

"Yeah, Brant's got a talent with oral."

"No question," Jaxx gasps, his chest rising and falling in quick, shallow breaths. "I'm almost done my turn."

A rush of pre-cum slicks my Brant-tossing hand and I smear it on the shaft. "I get to suck on you as soon as Jaxx is finished, Bear. You promised me some sixty-nine action."

"Mhmm," Brant moans.

"Okay, stop," Jaxx says, pulling free. "Any more and I'm going to come so hard I spill straight into your stomach. You two get into position, I've got designs on Brant's ass."

I giggle and Brant waggles his brows. "Well, alrighty then, Jaguar. Who am I to argue? You do you."

Jaxx

One thing I love about our quint is that everyone is game for anything at any time. With my release pushing at the head of my cock, I need to get strategic. This wooden cube of privacy may have walls and a makeshift bed, but it doesn't have lube.

And I want Brant's ass.

I have just enough restraint to shift back and let the two of them get sorted. Brant lets off a sexy rumble as he faceplants in Calli's pussy and she lets off a feminine groan that makes it clear our girl is hot and hungry.

She wriggles her naked backside a little and then shifts her right arm between his massive, muscled thighs to grab hold and guide that thick arousal to her mouth.

The moment she sucks him in, his entire body shudders.

The sensation tingles hot in my balls.

Locked and loaded I grip tighter and stroke. Damn. The scent of Calli's need permeates the air and my wild side rises to the challenge. "Our wildcat is restless today, Bear. Looks like we need to tire her out."

Brant smiles over his shoulder at me, his lips glistening. "Good thing I've got a hearty appetite."

Fuck, that's sexy. I position myself behind him and get to business. This first release is pleasure with a greater purpose. The fun will begin after that.

I prime my pleasure, absorbing every moan and scent and image to get me off. When the pressure builds to the point of blowing my load, I line up with Brant's ass and rub my cock against his entrance.

He groans and presses back, and I love the enthusiasm.

My cum spills in lazy spurts and slicks him up good.

"Now we're in business." I don't worry about recovery. Wildlings have fast refractory times and by the time I've got him stretched and primed for the next event, I'll be as hard as a marble column.

Slicking through my mess, I draw a thumb down the crevice of his crack and play with the tight ring of his anus.

He groans again and pushes against my ministrations.

"Calli's not the only one hot and hungry."

Brant's too busy to acknowledge me. I ease back a few inches and look straight down. Calli's eyes are closed and she's absorbed in her task.

With my thumb still inside him, I grab the globe of his ass and then do the same thing with my other hand on the other cheek. Once I've got both thumbs inside him, I start to stretch his muscles and moisten my path.

Calli lets off a cry of release and I ease off for a second to give him time to focus. After she starts to calm, I'm in business. "Ready or not…"

I push forward, breaching the initial resistance and sliding forward in a moist glide. That first, tight slide is my favorite. I get off on the rest, don't get me wrong, but the alpha in me loves that rush of power. Forcing that last bit of resistance to relax and accept me and what I want.

Focusing on pleasuring Brant, I slick things up with a few slow and deep penetrations and then build momentum. Brant's been a player for years and he can take this like a fucking trooper and not lose his load.

It doesn't take long before I'm pounding home and he has to brace his palms against the bed. I might feel bad for Calli having to pause what she's doing, but I know our girl. She'll be getting off on having a front-row view of me fucking Brant senseless.

And yeah, I can do this all day long.

Sweat drips from my brow and my lungs start to burn. Sexing up my mates is a total body workout. Who needs a gym membership when you've got four mates?

Speaking of our mates… I access my mating bond and make sure it's lit up. Yeah, it's a dick thing to do when they're trying to be all master of the universe, but hey….

Mate sex trumps pixie politics.

The air is filled with the sounds of sex, flesh slapping, and the creak and groan of wood settling into its construction.

Life is good. All we need is for the others to get here.

CHAPTER SEVENTEEN

Kotah

My mates are insatiable. Here we are, working on my first act as Fae Prime, ironing out the ownership of what will arguably the most important facet of the two realms, and the mating bond connecting the five of us is thrumming with the erotic appetites of Calli, Jaxx, and Brant.

I cast a sideways glance at Hawk and yeah, he's feeling it too. He was standing and now is sitting on the ground, bent at the waist to disguise what's going on in his lap.

For fuck's sake, he grumbles in my mind. *They're like horny teenagers. Can't we be gone ten minutes without them stripping down and mounting one another?*

Honestly, I'd rather be there.

No shit. Yet here we are being the adults of the quint.

I bite my bottom lip and fight the groan as Brant's pleasure spikes. *Whatever Jaxx is doing to him... oh, who are we kidding, we both know what Jaxx is doing to him. I wish he was doing that to me.*

You and me both.

"Are you two even listening to me?" the queen asks.

Hawk lets off a heavy sigh and nods. "Apologies, Queen. We are sensing an influx of emotion through our mating connection. It's distracting, but nothing to be alarmed about. Where were we?"

"You know very well where we were, Barron. You are refusing to acknowledge my claim on the portal gate."

He smiles. "Because you don't own it, Majesty. The portal gate is on fae land and always has been. The FCO has the original surveys and deeds that go back centuries to prove it. Whether or not the river's course was intentionally altered to shift the boundaries, in no way do the pixies have grounds to lay claim to the gate."

The Queen bares her teeth, but Hawk seems unaffected.

He smiles and arches a brow. "And now that our official stance is clear, what is it you truly desire DenysTa? You don't need the money and I highly doubt you want travelers tromping on and off land you inhabit. What does claiming the gate get you in the long run?"

"So cynical, Barron."

Hawk chuckles. "We're cut from the same cloth, Queen. You're a shrewd leader and wouldn't have gone to all this trouble simply to stir up a fuss."

The queen draws a pointed claw down the column of her neck and grins. "Perhaps there is a way for you to repay my custodianship of the gate property."

Hawk smiles and folds his fingers together in his lap. "Well, the Fae Prime and I were saying yesterday only the most gifted and forward-thinking members of our realm would've anticipated the need to protect this location as much as a decade ago. You needed to figure out how to alter the location off FCO property—if in perception only—and ally with the Forest Lord and the fire dervishes."

The queen frowns. "What do you know of it?"

Hawk chuckles and holds out his open palms. "My dear friend, you've known me long enough to realize I know everything that goes on in the realm. The Forest Lord needed a home and a race of fae to help him remain hidden while he tried to open the gate. The dervishes took him in. The Black Knight caught him up in his web, things went off the rails."

"That Black Knight is a meddlesome and vicious man. He took our tree man and ruined everything."

Hawk nods. "I'm sure he did, but he's dead now and the portal rift is open. In a matter of days, the bridge will be established, and this area will be overrun with curious fae."

"What's your point?"

"You have the Fae Prime sitting here with you and he's grateful you protected the gate and would welcome negotiations with the pixies to reward your great race for your efforts. What would you ask of him?"

The Queen of Pixies stands on the mossy stump and raises her chin. "I demand a seat on the Fae Counsel. For too long, the diminutive and lesser fae races have been ignored. We want a voice."

That's an easy one. "Done. I agree. And as your first royal duty, I would like you to parley with the leaders of other diminutive races and let me know what's been overlooked by my father. Tell me where the political system is failing you and the members of the communities like yours."

Queen DenysTa looks stunned at first. She stares at me with her mouth open and then gathers her wits. "Thank you, Highness. Thy will be done."

"Good then. Is there anything else?"

She looks at the trees and it's obvious she's thinking up other things she might get out of me. I don't care. Whether it was her or the Forest Lord who moved the river, it allowed us to fulfill our destiny and reestablish a gate opening.

Once we get the bridge established, the Fae Realms will be united. Once these negotiations are over, I can get naked with my mates.

"The pixies shall get a royal tribute erected at the gate telling of our foresight and efforts in preserving the site and making it possible to unite the realms."

"Agreed."

Her smile grows and she puffs up a little more. "And you and your mates will feast with us once a year and hear our thoughts on the realm."

"Agreed."

"And—"

Hawk is reading something off his phone and jolts to his feet. "Excuse us, Majesty, but we need to go."

"Go?" She flaps her wings and stomps her clawed

talons against her perch. "What is more important than my final arrangements with the Fae Prime?"

He finishes reading his screen and looks at me. "Jaxx just texted. The bridge is established, and the gate has activated."

"Activated? Your man said it would take days yet. What has he done?"

"It wasn't him, DenysTa. The bridge was established from the StoneHaven side… and someone's coming through."

Jaxx

I fall to the bedding platform breathing heavy and drained from a strenuous round of mate fukery when I notice the hammering and sawing have stopped. Instead of the droning sounds of construction, men are shouting outside our home.

"Jaxx? What's wrong?" Calli asks, rousing from the golden glow of post-coitus bliss.

"Shit," Brant says, rolling to his feet. "It's something."

The bear tosses me my jeans and I pull them up my thighs in a rush. There's no time for buttoning up or shirts. Brant and I launch out our front door, barefoot and barely dressed.

Lukas is backing away from the fluctuating fae magic that surrounds the gate. He points to us. "Text Barron and get him here now. Someone activated the gate. We're about to have visitors."

"Oh, shit." I rush back inside, grab my phone, and send the text as Calli throws on Brant's shirt and joins me outside the cabin door.

"What's happening?"

"That." I pull her to the side as the energy of the gate surges and a shrieking scream explodes in the air. I let go of Calli to press my palms against my ears and wince as the noise vibrates in my skull.

Calli clamps her ears and doubles over too.

What the hell is it?

I straighten in time to see two massive, winged beasts fly through the undulating power of the portal. They're black and green and if it wasn't impossible, I'd swear they are—

"Dragons!" Calli screeches, taking shelter behind the tree. "You never said anything about dragons!"

Shit. "I didn't know."

The mythical monsters push above the canopy of trees, flap their great, scaled wings, and circle.

"So, this happened," Brant says, rushing in to join us. "Let's see Hawk's people conceal that."

I blink at our bear. "We *are* Hawk's people, numbnut. So, yeah, what should we do?"

"Do they come in peace?"

The dragons have rebounded and are coming in hot. When they open their mouths and breathe streams of blue fire at us, Brant's question is answered.

Before we have time to react, Calli bursts into flame and launches into the air. She blocks their fire and screams a shrill fury.

Hawk and Kotah arrive as the battle begins. "Fuck me," Hawk says. "Dragons? Seriously?"

"Seems so."

"Incoming." Lukas braces his stance and aims his gun at the pulsing gate.

"Fuck this," Brant says, flipping into his bear form.

Kotah and I follow his lead.

Hawk draws his guns and has both hands poised and ready to fire. When the invader comes through, Brant charges and goes in hard. The wolf and I are tight on his ass.

The beast that comes through this time is a Brant-sized wolf. Shimmering midnight blue with opal eyes, it's a wild and fearsome monster.

Brant takes him to the ground and the thing seems surprised. It recovers quickly though, and the fight is on.

Kotah and I are looking for a way in when a fourth comes through. This time, it's a woman. She's mauve-skinned with raven black hair that hangs in spiral tendrils to the silk bodice of her gown. She's thin to the point of gauntness and her features are angular and harsh. Emerging into the clearing, she frowns at the ensuing chaos.

"Stop this! How dare you attack us."

Kotah flips back to his human form and now I'm torn.

Do I back up Brant against the beast or Kotah? Hawk answers for me and moves in to act as the welcome delegation. Good. I wanted to join the fight anyway. I jump on the demon wolf and sink my claws in its neck. It lets off an unholy scream and I admit, it's very satisfying.

As we pin the beast to the ground, one of the

dragons is thrown to the forest floor. Its wings fold and take out a row of trees. Pixies and fire dervishes scatter and scream.

I check the sky and Calli's got the other dragon in a fiery grasp and is fighting mid-air.

This shit is getting good.

Kotah

I straighten before the enraged female and gauge her intentions. She's not a wildling. She's one of the magical races by the feel of her energy. "I am Queen Laryssa of Dornte and I demand this stop."

I lift my chin and meet her gaze. "I am Nakotah Northwood, Fae Prime of this realm, and your beasts attacked us."

"Impossible. They were told to secure the area for first contact."

"They opted to do that by force. We responded in kind."

Calli flings the second dragon to the ground. It hits the earth in a staggering thud and lets off a pitiful howl.

Jaxx and Brant have the oversized wolf creature pinned and are tearing at it with their fangs.

"Stop! Release my son!"

Hawk stands at my hip and scowls. "If I stop our defenses, do I have your word the violence ends?"

"You do," the queen says.

Hawk closes his eyes and I feel him access our internal communication channel. *Enough for now, guys. We've made our point.*

The queen looks at the mangled mess of her front-line offense and scowls. "Is this the welcome we get after centuries of being separated?"

Kotah shrugs. "It didn't have to be. We were ready to greet you with welcome until your dragons attacked."

The two winged monsters make their way to the downed wolf and all three of them shift form.

"Are they wildlings?" I ask. "We don't have their species within our wildling races here."

The queen frowns. "There is much to learn about both worlds, I'm sure. For now, may I get my idiot son and his guards some medical care? I would hate to see them perish and our first encounter is a declaration of war."

"Of course," I say, searching the scrub for the backpack. "I'll see to it straight away."

In a small, zipped pocket of my pack, I find a clear vial that contains Calli's tears from the other day. I hand that off to Jaxx and the fire-proof dress off to Brant. "Did you see where she landed?"

Brant nods. "I've got her."

With that taken care of, I get back to our first contact. "Shall we try again? Queen Laryssa of Dornte, welcome to the Human Realm."

She straightens and seems to take the do-over offer as intended. "Much better, young Nakotah. That is how you welcome a queen."

Calli chuckles beside me as she and Brant join us. "And did you miss the part about him being the Fae Prime and King of the fae on this side of the gate?"

Laryssa smiles. "No dear. I'm sure for what this

realm has faced, this boy might've been sufficient as a leader, but now that we're uniting, I assure you, I am the more suitable leader."

I frown and my wolf lets off a long, low growl. "If you think you can saunter through the gate that *we* opened into the realm that *I* rule and tell us how the future will unfold, it's you who is mistaken. I might not know what StoneHaven has faced the past centuries, but neither do you know anything of this realm."

"On the contrary," she says. "I have been sending travelers here for years, keeping tabs on the other half of my queendom. Now, tell me, where is Sabastian Barron Whitehouse. I must speak with him."

As Hawk's name is spoken a wave of goosebumps prickle my skin. "I'm Sabastian Whitehouse... but I don't use that name anymore."

She looks him over and frowns. "You're not how I pictured you."

"Oh? And how exactly is that?"

Her gaze narrows on him and she seems to find what she sees displeasing. "From what my people said, you're a wealthy, self-made billionaire with power and allies and systems in place that will help me rule."

He blinks. "I am all those things, but as Nakotah mentioned, you're not coming here to rule. This realm has established leadership in place and our system works well. It would be my pleasure to liaise with the leaders from your realm and help with integration and both immigration and emigration, but we didn't open this gate to be overthrown... and quite frankly, it's presumptuous for you to think it possible."

Well said, hotness, Jaxx says. *Do you think her people were talking about your father and not you?*

My insides tighten. I thought of that but hoped that wasn't the case.

It makes more sense than her bursting to meet me.

Calli frowns. *If she's aligned with him, that casts a serious shadow on her, doesn't it?*

I don't disagree, kitten, but whether or not she's speaking about Hawk or his father, we don't have any proof that she's even the authority of the other realm.

Agreed, for all that we know she's a poser who happened to come through the portal first.

I'm with Calli, Brant says. *Maybe the real leaders are at the other end of the Kansas portal and have no idea we've managed to open things up.*

Hawk's dark brow tightens. *There's too much we don't know. We can't make any decisions until we're sure.*

I straighten as the three men who emerged through the portal in a flurry come to join us. *And FYI, the queen wasn't at all annoyed with her envoys for coming through the portal and starting a fight. She was only angry that they lost.*

Good to know, Wolf. Let's not rush into offering her a key to the city just yet.

Agreed. I take a deep breath and project what I hope is the image of a confident ruler. "We've only just begun building the portal gate facilities. Let me introduce you to DenysTa, Queen of Pixies. And this is my mother, Malayna Northwood, up until my coronation, she was the Queen of this realm for almost twenty years."

"And when was your coronation, child?" she says, her tone patronizing.

"Only days ago."

She chuckles. "Well then, this established leadership your man boasted of is non-existent. The blood of your sacrifices has barely grown cold. Therefore, I restate my intention to assume responsibility for both realms."

Going back to where the backpacks are, I select a very specific duffle and bring it to the group. "If we must do this, I restate my intention and make my position very clear."

I set the bag on the ground before the supposed queen of the fae realm and straighten. "You asked where Sabastian Whitehouse is, and this is he," I gesture to Hawk, "but I believe you might be referring to Sabastian Whitehouse Senior, his father. He was recently involved in an illegal coup d'etat."

I bend and unzip the bag, gripping the hair of Hawk's father to lift the severed head into the air. "His plan ended badly."

The queen's gaze tightens and the acrid scent of her rage and disappointment is more satisfying than I would've thought possible.

"So, if this billionaire, all-powerful, highly connected ally of yours is the reason you came at me with dismissive arrogance, we need to solidify a new understanding. Your plans to sweep in and conquer this realm were fueled by a villainous saboteur. Being misled left you misinformed. You've been set straight now, so we either move forward and discuss the two realms or you gather your wounded and go back where you came from."

Well said, Wolf. Hawk says. *You kicked her ass.*

I see the love and support in the looks from Brant, Calli, and Jaxx, and Hawk's words sink in. Yeah, I did kick her ass.

Round one, anyway.

I'm the motherfucking Fae Prime and while I never wanted it, I'll be damned if some stranger is going to waltz in and take it from me.

As Calli would say, 'yeah-no, don't think so.'

"Shall we go somewhere and talk? The site is in its infancy, but I'm sure my mates and I can find somewhere comfortable. Mother, would you care to join us? I think your experience and wisdom as former Queen of this realm makes you ideal counsel for what's to come."

Mother steps out of the shadows and presses a hand on my wrist. For the first time in my life, the contact isn't painful. My omega gift picks up her emotions and for the first time in my life, she's proud of me.

I swallow, raise my chin, and gesture for the group to proceed. The portal gate is active and there is much to do.

CHAPTER EIGHTEEN

Calli

Kotah never ceases to amaze me. He has the mind of a scholar and the instincts of a leader. While he and Hawk tackle the task of making inroads with her almighty pompous ass Queen Laryssa of Dornte. Jaxx, Brant, and I take on the three young men sitting on the ground enjoying the show.

"So, dragons, eh? And twins, that's cool."

That comment earns me a heated glare.

The twins are tall, broad, blond, Viking-type young men with long shaggy hair that hangs over their eyes. I have no idea what color their eyes are. They're like young Thor warriors… just take away the hammer and exchange it with the ability to become fire-breathing, flying reptiles. And they're identical… like seriously can't tell them apart.

"And what? You're guardians of the prince here?" I gesture to the demon wolf boy, Prince Creed of Dornte.

Now that he's not in the form of a massive demon wolf, Creed is quite handsome in a dark and broody sort of way. He looks nothing like the queen. His skin isn't mauve and his features are chiseled without being angular. He has the same angry and guarded gaze as Hawk and the same wounded soul vibe as Kotah.

Hang that on a twenty-two-year-old, ripped bod and give him a mane of silver hair, and voila, Prince Creed.

Funny, before being resurrected, I never realized how many wounded people roamed the earth.

Not really funny. Just funny I didn't notice.

"So, not an overly chatty bunch." I shrug and take a seat on the log by the fire. "Yes, we beat the snot out of you, but we can still be friends."

"Sleck off."

I blink. "Sweet, they do speak."

Jaxx chuckles and crosses his ankles. "My suggestion, boys, do not piss us off. We're neighbors now. Instead, ask and answer questions. We worked for months to open this rift and honestly, your lack of appreciation is underwhelming."

"You didn't beat us," one of the twins says.

I chuckle. "Oh, yeah. I totes did. Tomorrow, if you want a rematch, we can try again. Maybe I won't let them use my tears to heal you, though. Maybe a little suffering would humble you up a bit."

That earns me a couple of impressive scowls.

"So, you are an honest to gods phoenix," one of the dragon twins says.

"Yep. And you two are twin dragons. I *do* think that's cool. Do you have cool matchy names or anything?"

"No."

"So, do I get to know your names?"

"No."

"Alrighty then. Good talk." They eye each other and shrug. It's kinda funny. Watching them is like sitting in a funhouse and having the mirror reflect two identical images at me.

"Their names are Vikarus and Rhylan, or Vik and Rhy to their friends."

"Which you're not," one of them snaps.

"Understood, dragon boy." I raise my palms and try to come up with another line of questioning. "So, the realm you're from. Is it all fae and magical creatures?"

They look at me like that's a bizarre question.

It's the prince who answers. "As opposed to what?"

"Well, I was born and raised human, and then I transitioned to a wildling and was reborn. I was wondering if the entire population of your realm is fae and magical or if you have… I don't know, non-magicals, or aliens, or sea creatures or something. Help a girl out. I'm trying to start a convo."

"How about we don't?"

My eyebrows raise and I shrug. "Fine. Consider that over. Sulk all you want, broody boys. I was trying to be nice."

"No one's nice for no reason."

I roll my eyes. "Maybe in your world. In this world, most people are nice and the ones who aren't are the exception."

"What the fiery karnos is that?" One of the twins says, pointing at the sky.

I blink, watching the white stream of cloud cross

above us. "It's an airplane." They throw me a blank stare, so I elaborate. "It's a vehicle to travel long journeys through the air."

The twins laugh. "That's what wings are for."

I chuckle. "Yes, but here in the human realm, only birds, bats, and airplanes have wings. There are no such things as dragons or phoenix or pixies in this realm. We live secretly among the humans and can't have you two soaring through the sky."

"A great reason to go home."

"But you just got here."

Creed pegs me with a sardonic smile. "You have a touch of asshole in you, you know that?"

"Thanks. I work at it."

That gets me a slight smirk. "What about food? Do prisoners get to eat in this realm?"

I chuckle. "You're not our prisoners. We're just shooting the shit. If you want food, help yourself. But understand, if you try anything, we're ready and very willing to kick your asses."

Creed glares at me and his emotions lockdown. "Watch yourself, phoenix. You might have bested us in your full, warrior form, but as a female, you're weak and vulnerable to any number of attacks."

The growls that vibrate in the air around us are all menace and warning. They come from Brant and Jaxx but also Keyla and Doc.

Creed rolls his eyes and stands. "I take it by how much the brute here has eaten that it's not poisoned?"

I chuckle. "No. If we wanted you dead, you'd be dead."

"Did you guys really cut off the head of the other guy's father?" Creed asks, his back to us as he's amassing a plate of food that Brant would be proud of.

"It happened," I say, not willing to get into it. "Did your mother really think she could send you three in and overtake our realm?"

"She's not my mother," Creed says, glaring back at me, his eyes flipping to the opal glow of his demon wolf.

"Easy," Jaxx snaps. "Down, boy."

The dragon twins launch to their feet to back up their prince and Keyla and Doc shift as they join us and step in beside me.

Creed turns around, locks gazes with Keyla and the two of them fall limp to the forest floor.

"What the fuck?" Doc says, dropping to examine her.

"What did you do to him," one of the twins shouts.

"Nothing," I say, rushing to check on the kid. "I didn't instigate simultaneous fainting."

"Well then, what happened?" one of them asks while the other one checks over his shoulder.

"Creed, wake up. If she comes back and sees you like this, we're all dead. Come on. Get up."

I doubt it's the urging of the Viking boys that brings the prince around, but he and Keyla wake at the same time. It's freaky actually. At the same moment, the two of them snap awake and sit up.

"Are you okay, girlfriend?" I ask, not liking the look on her face one bit.

Tears pool in her eyes as she stands. Creed matches

her stance and looks almost as upset. She turns, looking toward the portal gate. "I'm sorry." She looks at Doc and her tears fall. "I'm sorry."

Keyla launches into the air, shifting on the fly as Creed does the same. Jaxx, Doc, and Brant all shout and burst into the chase, but a second later a white wolf and a midnight blue demon wolf are diving at the rift.

I blink when they pass right through the ebbing magic and land in the clearing. I catch up to Jaxx and the others and they look as confused as I do. "What happened. Why are they still here?"

Lukas is there. He's scowling and shakes his head. "I shut the bridge down. We already have one hostile queen, two dragons, and a demon shifter. I figured that's enough surprises for one day."

"You're the man, Lukas," Jaxx says, holding up his palms toward the two wolves snarling at us. "Any ideas on what we do about them?"

Lukas shakes his head. "None."

"There's nothing you can do," Mallory says, coming out of another one of the wooden cube tiny houses in progress. The hulderfolk male is still wearing his FCO security uniform but his tail is uncoiled, and he looks different somehow. "Those two are soul seared."

"What the fuck does that mean, little man," Doc snaps. "What did he do to her?"

"He did nothing. It's something that happens. Two souls mirrored so perfectly that when they stand face to face, they are bound for life. It's irreversible."

I run a hand over my face as the blood drains from my head. Hawk said Mallory was unable to lie, but how can this be true. "They're strangers… and from different realms… and Keyla and Doc are together…"

Devastation and fury war in Doc's gaze and my heart is breaking for him.

"We'll figure this out." Even as I hear the words, I'm not sure how I can even say that. "Mallory, maybe you're mistaken. How can you be so sure this is a soul searing thing?"

"Because I'm soul seared." He shrugs, his smile sympathetic. "You'll see. When they shift back, they'll wear a mating mark. It's quite wonderful. Something to celebrate."

Doc's black bear weighs in on that and I sigh. "Maybe we should hold off on the champagne for a bit."

Hawk

Turmoil screaming on the mating bond brings Kotah and me to attention and turning. "Forgive us, ladies. Something is very wrong. We're needed back at the clearing." I meet the gaze of the security detail watching over the queens and tilt my head to signal them to move in to escort them.

Then, the two of us run through the trees to get back to our mates. I don't know if it's part of the mating magic or if simply in tune with them, but even in a forest, as I'm rounding the fire, with a crowd of people gathering, I can pick my mates out easily.

"Well, they're alive and standing."

"Then what's wrong?"

"The baby?"

"I don't think so."

As we draw nearer, Calli turns. She looks heartbroken, her attention focused on Kotah.

"What is it, *Chigua*?" he asks, his voice tight.

She tells us about Keyla and Creed and them collapsing and what Mallory said about their souls recognizing one another. "They tried to go through the portal but when they couldn't they got all growly. Now she won't shift back and he's keeping everyone from getting to her."

Kotah is the Fae Prime and crowds part when he approaches. We're soon front and center, looking at two very irate wolves. One beautiful and white. The other, three times the normal size, midnight blue with eerie opal eyes.

We referred to the prince as a demon wolf, but honestly, I don't know what he is or how he got this way.

A tug on my shirtsleeve brings my attention to Mallory. "I'm sorry, sir. I didn't mean to upset your mates."

"Not your fault, my friend. Wow, it's a heck of a first day for you to manage the portal gate, though."

He nods. "You promised it would be an exciting change of pace and you were right, sir."

I chuckle. "It's been that for sure. Do you have any idea how to calm them down so they'll shift back? We're not going to get much sorted out with them snarling and snapping at anyone who comes near them."

"When my mate and I were Soul Seared, it took weeks until we felt ourselves again."

Weeks? "Alright, thank you, Mallory."

Queen Laryssa and the Prima catch up to us and I explain the best I can. Neither of them takes it well, so I leave them to freak out and go to Calli. I feel her worry and anxiety so sharply across the mating bond and it hurts.

"Hey, Spitfire."

Calli hugs me. "Is everyone caught up?"

"I think so." I assess the two snarling wolves, Kotah trying to approach, Calli beside herself, Brant trying to talk Doc down, and Jaxx wrangling two dragon wildlings and I'm thankful not to have to take the world on alone anymore.

This is us now. A team. This is our quint.

Kotah

It's late when Hawk, Brant, and I shed our clothes and crawl onto the foam mattress with Calli and Jaxx. At some point during the day, Lukas found us linens and pillows. Honestly, I'm so tired I wouldn't have cared if I had to sleep on a stone floor.

"Hey, sweet prince," Calli says, her voice heavy with sleep. "How's the latest disaster?"

It took over an hour to calm Keyla and Creed enough to get them into one of the wooden shacks that will soon be temporary housing for fae travelers. It took another hour to talk Doc down from stomping in there and inserting himself into the confusion. The dragon twins are wound up. The queens are freaking out. And all I want to do is curl up with my mates and shut out the world until morning.

"The fires are put out for tonight. Hawk's people are

in place and will let us know if anything changes. I'm scared to death about Keyla, but I can't think about it anymore."

"Then you came to the right place, my man," Jaxx says, reaching over Calli's hip to caress my waist. There's no light and no windows, but my wolf's night vision makes it easy to see. "Consider this a sexy safe zone. No thinking allowed."

I chuckle as Brant snuggles up behind me and Hawk settles behind Jaxx. Calli runs a gentle touch along my jaw and cups my cheek. "Do you want to sleep or would you prefer some sexual comfort?"

"Is that a real question?"

The guys chuckle.

Calli frowns. "Hey, there's nothing wrong with being polite and asking. He could be too tired or stressed. It was his first day ruling and a lot happened."

"You did a great job," Hawk says, his hand draping casually over Jaxx's hip and stroking him in a lazy pull. "I'm proud of you, Kotah. We all are."

"Yes, we are," Calli says, rolling onto her hip so we're chest-to-chest. The rounds of her breasts press against the flat planes of mine and I'm struck by the knowledge that my beloved girls are going to grow over the next months. A woman's breasts grow bigger and fuller in the months of pregnancy. I can hardly wait.

I slide my hand up the bumpy ridges of her ribcage and cup the mound of her breasts. Her nipples are tight and extended and I give them a gentle pinch.

Calli's head drops back and she groans. "In honor of your successes, you rule the hour, sweet prince. What would you like to do? Any ideas?"

"Decisions. Decisions. Where to begin."

Jaxx

If you've ever lived through a chain of events where one thing after another goes off the rails and you wonder what's happening around you, why, and when it will stop so you can catch your breath, then you know what I mean when I say…

Life is crazy.

Three months ago, the universe sucker-punched the five of us. Yeah, we took more than a few hits, but we fought to keep ahead of the storm.

Now, it's happening again… this time to Keyla.

As a male who's always had a passion for life, for love, and the world around me, I never expected I'd be named a guardian of a mythical firebird, have four hot and amazing mates, and end up with a baby on the way.

Somehow, life gives you everything you never knew you needed. I only hope Keyla is as fortunate… and Doc.

Poor Doc.

But there's no telling. Like I said… life is crazy.

Three months ago Calli died on the graveled shoulder on the side of the road.

It was the end and the beginning.

Because that's when our lives truly began.

~~ THE END ~~

Thank you for reading Jaguar's Passion the fifth and final book in Calli's harem. Don't panic, there's more coming. As Keyla's family, the quint will be an integral part of the cast in the next harem. Plus, Calli needs to figure out about Riley. *Annnd* there's a baby coming.

I have every intention of allowing you all to follow their stories and when the time comes… there will be additional scenes and content from the perspective of Calli, Jaxx, Kotah, Hawk, and Brant so that you can share all the feels with them.

I hope you're ready for the next installment as we explore what happens now that the portal gate is open and the realms are open for business.
Claim book 6 – Dark Curse now.

If you are inclined to help a girl out, it would be amazing if you could leave a star rating or review on Amazon.

If you want more, join my newsletter and be notified when new books launch and for all my news and sales!

Author Notes

Written on 10/29/2020

Thank you so much for reading, and since you're reading this—for continuing to read. I value your time and am thankful Calli, Kotah, Hawk, Brant, and Jaxx meant enough to you to finish the first series in the Guardians of the Fae Realms Series.

Guardians of the Fae Realms doesn't end here. Follow along with this cast of characters as Calli's pregnancy progresses and her search for Riley continues.

What's in store for Keyla and Doc now that Creed is in the picture? How will Kotah's days as Fae Prime shape up. Will they get back to the chicken nacho night and Jaxx's next sex game?

Find out in Book 6 – Dark Curse - Keyla's harem.

Hugs to all,
JL

If you're a music person, songs might evoke images of people and situations in your mind. It does for me. Here are a couple that spoke loud and clear for me in the mindset of the characters. Close your eyes and see if you agree:

Cain Brown – What Ifs
Dean Brody – Whiskey in a Teacup
Tenille Townes – Somebody's Daughter
Thomas Rhett – Don't Threaten Me With A Good Time
Thomas Rhett – Blesssed
La Roux – Bulletproof,
Elvis Presley – Little Less Conversation

Social Media – You can find me on Amazon, Facebook, Twitter, Instagram, and through my Newsletter

JL's Email – jlmadorewrites@gmail.com

My web page – www.jlmadore.com

Guardians of the Fae Realms (Reverse Harem)

Calli's Harem

Book 1 – Rise of the Phoenix

Book 2 – Wolf's Soul

Book 3 – Bear's Strength

Book 4 – Hawk's Heart

Book 5 – Jaguar's Passion

Keyla's Harem

Book 6 – Dark Curse

Book 7 – Dark Soul

Book 8 – Dark Crown

The Watchers of the Gray Series (Paranormal Romance)

Book 1 – Watcher Untethered (Zander)

Book 2 – Watcher Redeemed (Kyrian)

Book 3 – Watcher Reborn (Danel)

Book 4 – Watcher Divided (Phoenix)

Book 5 – Watcher United (Seth)

Book 6 – Watcher Compelled (Bo)

Book 7 – Watcher Unfeigned (Brennus)

Book 8 – Watcher Exposed (Hark)

The Scourge Survivor Series (Urban Fantasy Romance)

Book 1 – Blaze Ignites

Book 2 – Ursa Unearthed

Book 3 – Torrent of Tears